W9-BRA-379

SUPER HEROES
STORYBOOK COLLECTION
MARVEL
NEW YORK

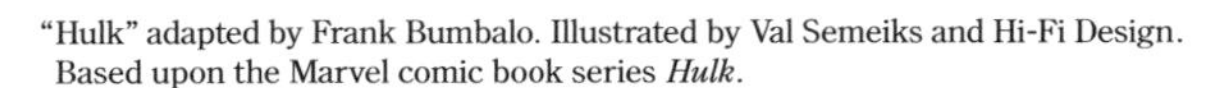
"Hulk" adapted by Frank Bumbalo. Illustrated by Val Semeiks and Hi-Fi Design. Based upon the Marvel comic book series *Hulk*.

"Iron Man" adapted by Tomas Palacios. Illustrated by Tom Grummett and Hi-Fi Design. Based upon the Marvel comic book series *Iron Man*.

"Spider-Man" adapted by Michael Siglain. Illustrated by The Storybook Art Group. Based upon the Marvel comic book series *Spider-Man*.

"Professor X" adapted by Clarissa Wong. Illustrated by The Storybook Art Group. Based upon the Marvel comic book series *The X-Men*.

"Dr. Strange" adapted by Bryan Q. Miller. Illustrated by Rick Burchett and Hi-Fi Design. Based upon the Marvel comic book series *Dr. Strange*.

"Black Widow" adapted by Alison Lowenstein. Illustrated by Mike Norton and Hi-Fi Design. Based upon the Marvel comic book series *The Avengers*.

"Ant-Man" adapted by Scott Peterson. Illustrated by Rick Burchett and Hi-Fi Design. Based upon the Marvel comic book series *The Avengers*.

"Captain America" adapted by Clarissa Wong. Illustrated by Val Semeiks, Hi-Fi Design, and The Storybook Art Group. Based upon the Marvel comic book series *Captain America*.

"Daredevil" adapted by Scott Peterson. Illustrated by Pat Olliffe and Hi-Fi Design. Based upon the Marvel comic book series *Daredevil*.

"Wasp" adapted by Scott Peterson. Illustrated by Rick Burchett and Hi-Fi Design. Based upon the Marvel comic book series *The Avengers*.

"The Original X-Men" adapted by Tomas Palacios. Illustrated by The Storybook Art Group. Based upon the Marvel comic book series *The X-Men*.

"Wolverine" adapted by Alison Lowenstein, Illustrated by Val Semeiks and Hi-Fi Design. Based upon the Marvel comic book series *Wolverine*.

"Fantastic Four" adapted by Alison Lowenstein, Illustrated by Pat Olliffe and Hi-Fi Design. Based upon the Marvel comic book series *The Fantastic Four*.

"Thor" adapted by Elizabeth Schaefer. Illustrated by The Storybook Art Group. Based upon the Marvel comic book series *Thor*.

"She-Hulk" adapted by Rich Thomas. Illustrated by Drew Johnson, Carlo Barberi, and Hi-Fi Design. Based upon the Marvel comic book series *She-Hulk*.

"Hawkeye" adapted by Alison Lowenstein. Illustrated by Mike Norton and Hi-Fi Design. Based upon the Marvel comic book series *The Avengers*.

"Spider-Woman" adapted by Rich Thomas. Illustrated by Pat Olliffe and Hi-Fi Design. Based upon the Marvel comic book series *Spider-Woman*.

"Silver Surfer" adapted by Nachie Castro. Illustrated by Pat Olliffe and Hi-Fi Design. Based upon the Marvel comic book series *The Fantastic Four*.

"All-New X-Men" adapted by Rich Thomas. Illustrated by Pat Olliffe and Hi-Fi Design. Based upon the Marvel comic book series *The X-Men*.

"The Avengers" adapted by Alison Lowenstein. Illustrated by Pat Olliffe and Hi-Fi Design. Based upon the Marvel comic book series *The Avengers*.

Printed in the United States of America

First Edition

1 3 5 7 9 10 8 6 4 2

G942-9090-6-13210

ISBN 978-1-4231-7223-9

Cover illustrated by Pat Olliffe, Val Semeiks, Mike Norton, Tom Grummett, Todd Nauck and Brian Miller

Storybook designed by Jennifer Redding

marvelkids.com

For Text Only

MARVEL

HULK

Hulk is the strongest there is. He can leap the farthest distances and lift the heaviest objects, and he cannot be hurt. Hulk can do the most incredible things. Yet, before the fateful day that Hulk came into being, he was just a man; a man by the name of Dr. Bruce Banner.

Bruce Banner had always dealt with bullies. His childhood was sad and lonely. Instead of dealing with his feelings, Bruce would bury himself in books. He became a doctor of science for the army. He studied a type of energy called gamma radiation. It was a dangerous energy source, but Bruce wanted to use it for the good of mankind. He knew the best way to test the power of the gamma rays was to cause a massive explosion.

General "Thunderbolt" Ross had other ideas for the use of gamma radiation. Ross was in charge of the army lab where Bruce worked. He reminded Bruce of the bullies he had faced throughout his life. General Ross was angry with Bruce, and lost his patience with the lack of results from the experiments. He needed results from Bruce, not excuses!

Bruce asked for more time to make sure the device was safe. He had to be sure no one would get hurt. General Ross became even angrier. He gave Bruce no choice; he had to listen to the general's orders.

Even though Bruce knew the device wasn't ready and could cause more harm than good, Bruce took the device into a safe area in the desert to be tested. He felt that he was being bullied once again.

Once the countdown began, Bruce noticed something on his computer screen. Looking through his telescope, he realized that someone had driven right into the danger zone! Bruce couldn't let anyone get hurt by his experiment! He rushed out of the lab and down to the test site.

It was a teenage kid and he was about to encounter a disaster! Bruce told the teenager in the car that he needed to get out of the car and get to safety right away.

Realizing they didn't have much time, he grabbed the boy out of the car and pushed him into a nearby shelter where he would be safe.

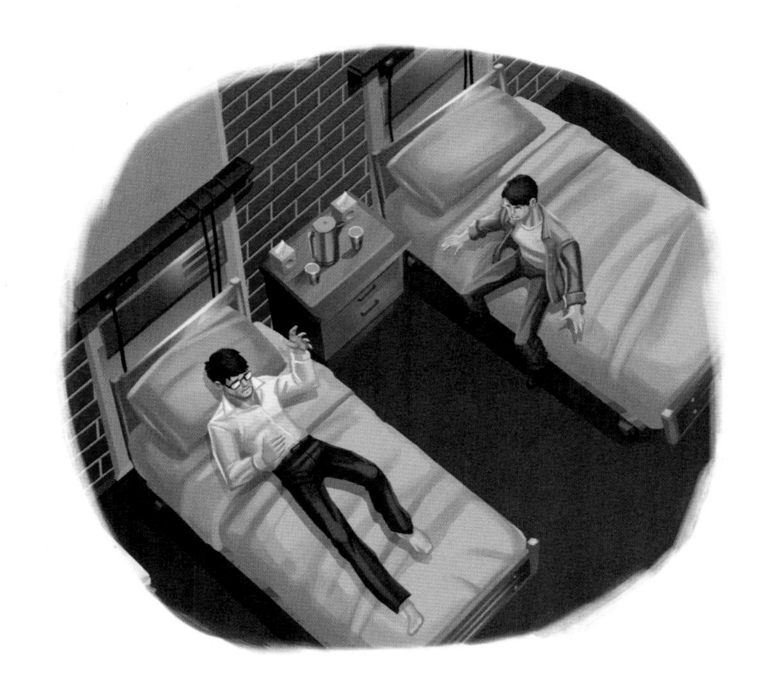

Bruce had saved the boy, but it was too late for him.

Bruce woke up in the military hospital. The teenager was in the bed next to his. He told Bruce his name was Rick Jones. Bruce was very happy that Rick was safe and sound. Rick was grateful to Bruce for saving his life. Bruce looked around the room and noticed all of the doors were locked. He began to panic; his heart was pumping fast, and he was scared!

Then Bruce began to change. The gamma rays had caused it. He grew twice his size and turned green from head to toe! He smashed through the wall to escape the room. The soldiers outside didn't recognize Bruce, so they began to attack him, calling him a HULK.

All Hulk wanted was to leave and to be left alone. He didn't want to hurt anyone. A tank began to fire on Hulk; he screamed "HULK SMASH!" and destroyed the cannon of the tank. But the tank had fired a shell. It hit the wall of the science lab where Bruce's team had been working.

Fire spread rapidly among all of the equipment. Most of the soldiers and scientists escaped, except for one soldier. He was trapped behind a wall of flame.

"Help me!" screamed the trapped solider. Hulk leaped toward the cries for help.

He pushed past the fire and rescued the solider, who thanked Hulk for saving his life.

Before the fighting could start again, and not wanting anyone else to get hurt, Hulk leaped into the hot desert. When he had gotten far enough away, he slowly transformed back into Bruce Banner.

Bruce was uncertain if he would ever become Hulk again, but he thought it would be safer to hide for a while. He needed time to think about what had happened. It was all so new to him.

Little did Bruce know at that time the impact Hulk would have on the world. Hulk would try his best to help those who couldn't help themselves.

That is why he's known as the INCREDIBLE HULK!

IRON MAN

Tony Stark had everything. He was an intelligent inventor. He was a billionaire. He ran a company called Stark Industries, which created powerful weapons that were used in war all over the world. But Tony's "perfect" life was about to change. . . forever.

One day, Tony went to a secret base to sell his high-tech weapons to the military. The military loved Tony's weapons because they were strong and powerful. Nobody made weapons like Tony.

Suddenly, they were attacked! A huge explosion blasted through the room, hurting Tony very badly.

An enemy army rushed in and quickly recognized the famous inventor. They grabbed Tony Stark and ran off. He had been kidnapped!

Tony was thrown into a dirty prison cell that was littered with mechanical parts and electronic equipment. The rebel army told Tony that he had been hurt in the blast and his heart had become weak. If Tony didn't help the rebels create a special weapon for them, he would not live very long. The inventor had no choice but to do what they demanded.

As Tony looked around, he noticed he wasn't alone. Another scientist by the name of Yinsen had also been captured and forced to work for the rebel army.

Tony and Yinsen began to draw various designs for weapons they thought the rebels would be interested in. . .

. . .Or so they wanted the rebels to think! In fact, the two scientists were making something not for the enemy force, but for themselves. Something that would help them escape.

The two scientists worked on their secret project for hours and hours. They cut metal into various shapes and sizes and heated the iron so that it could bend.

They made sure their invention was strong and powerful enough to withstand the enemy force when it attacked.

Finally, their device was finished. Tony and Yinsen then unleashed it—an iron suit—on the rebels and broke out of the prison!

Tony and Yinsen had escaped! They were safe and sound, and it was all because of the iron armor they had built.

Tony realized that he did not want to make weapons for war anymore. He wanted to protect people. That's when he got an idea! Tony Stark would help those in need. And he would use the iron suit to do it! In the armor, Tony could fight off villains and also soar through the sky.

But Tony knew that the clunky metal suit he had made out of spare parts wasn't the best invention. He needed to work out the kinks and clanks. Make it better. Make it lighter.

And with a powerful energy force called repulsor technology, Tony would make it—invincible!

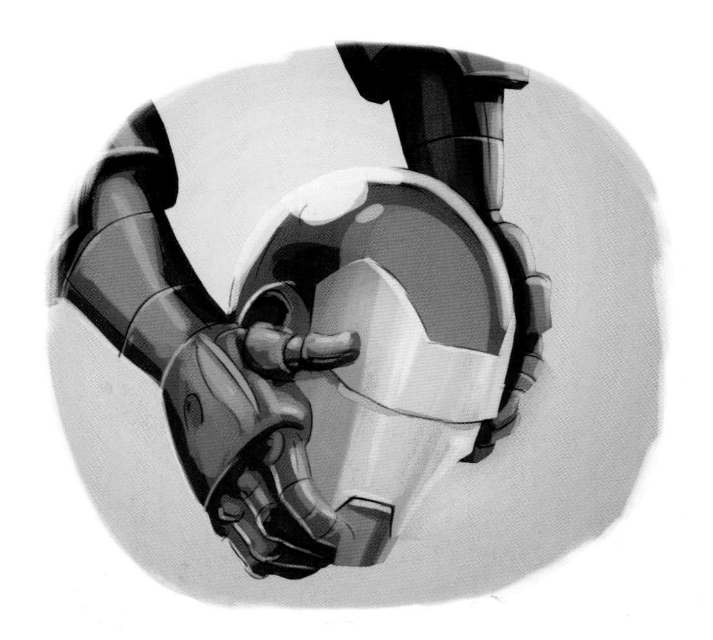

Tony changed the look of the armor, making it streamlined and smooth. And as long as Tony's special chest plate remained intact, his heart would beat strong. After making the final adjustments to the gloves, boots, and mask, Tony began to put on the parts piece by piece.

Finally, the man in the iron suit was ready! Tony had armor that was strong enough to protect those who needed it and stop those that wanted to bring fear to the world.

As Tony admired his shiny new suit, he heard a report come over the television that two super villains were attacking the downtown area. Tony knew that now was the time for the world to witness a new Super Hero in action.

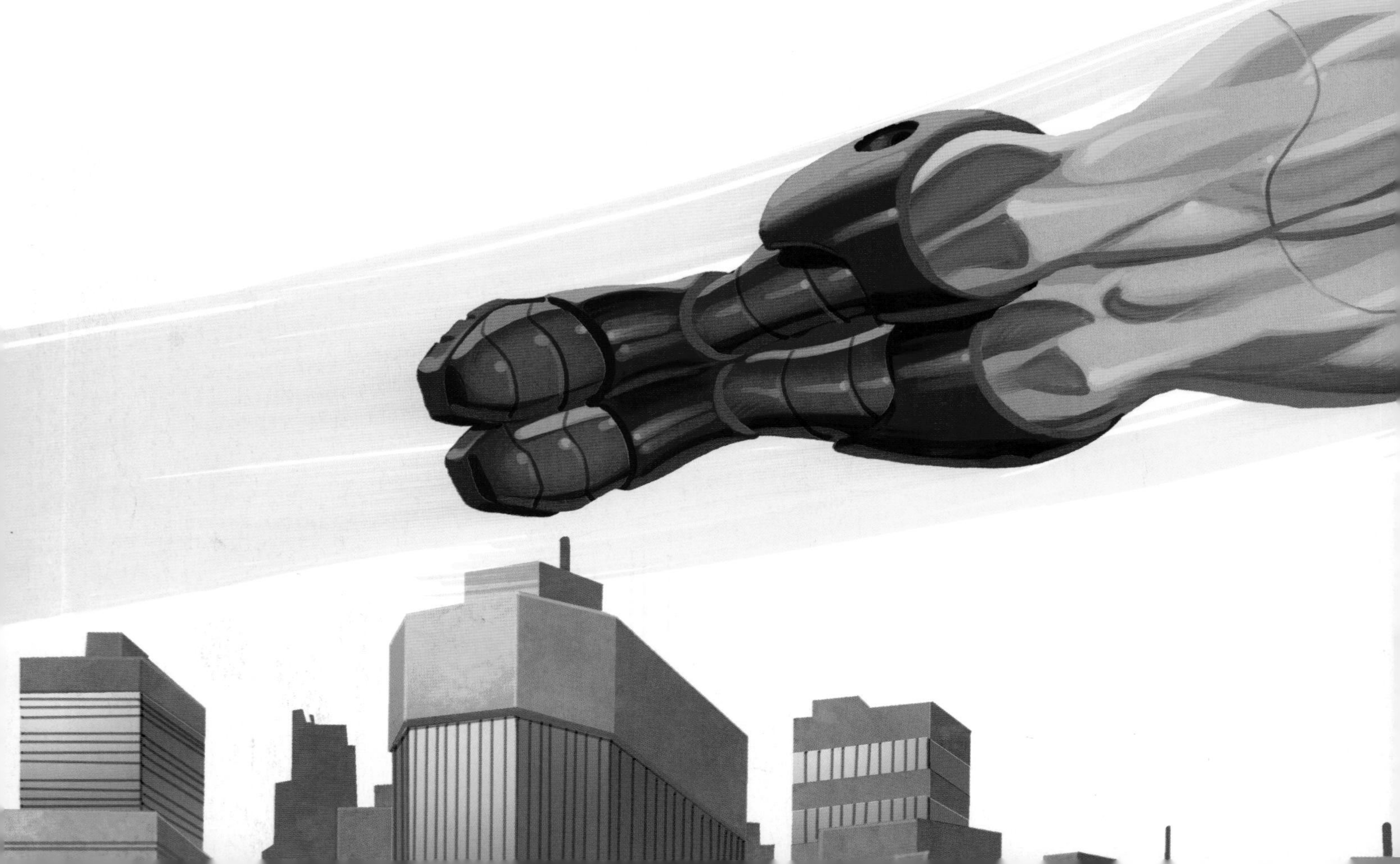

STARK

It was time for the world to witness the Invincible Iron Man!

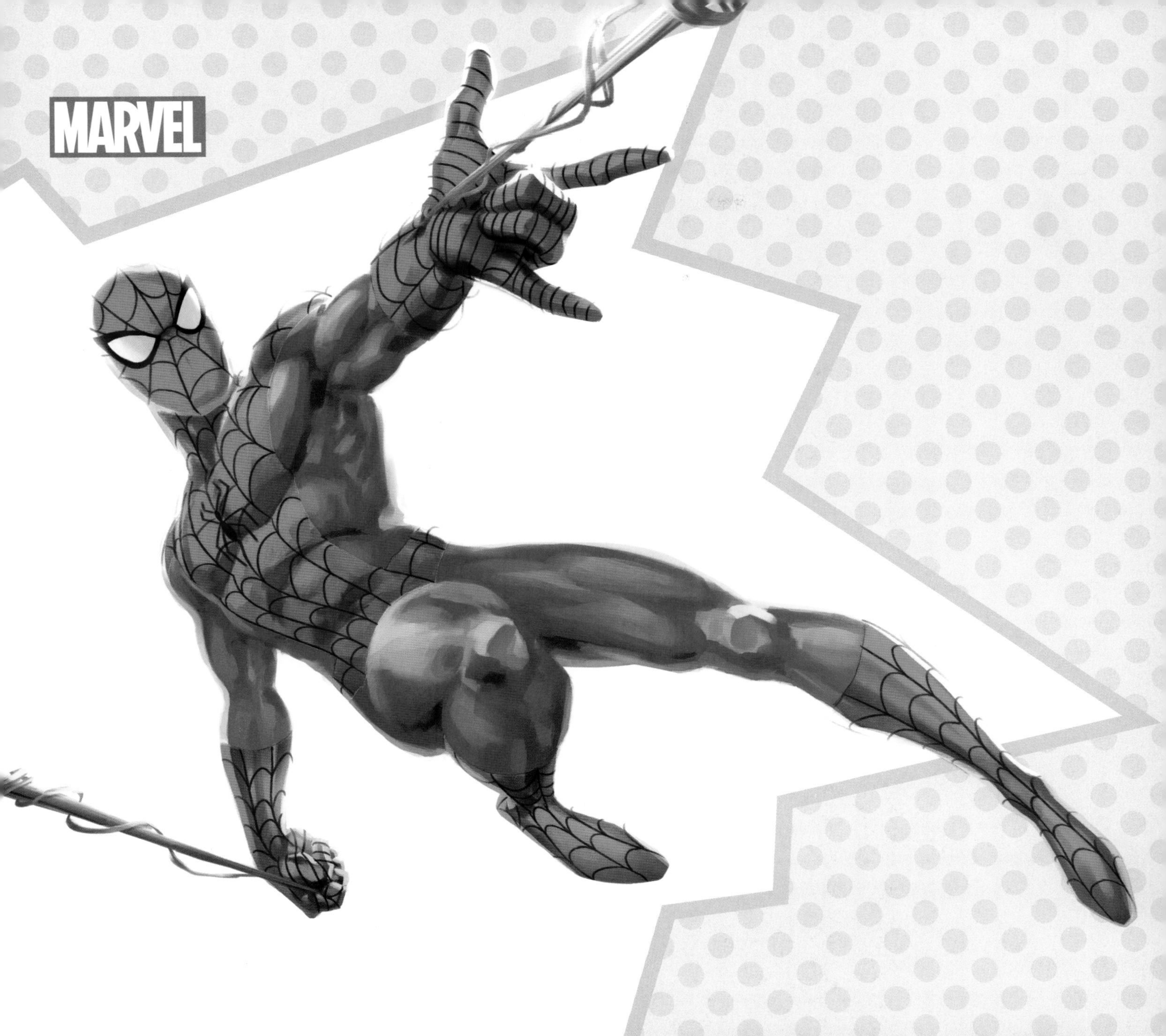

SPIDER-MAN

Peter Parker wasn't amazing, and he certainly wasn't a hero. Until he crossed paths with a radioactive spider, he was an average teenager who attended Midtown High School and lived in Queens, New York, with his uncle Ben and his aunt May.

Peter enjoyed school, especially science class. Although Peter loved to learn and study, he wasn't popular and was often bullied by the other students. Then one day, Peter's life was forever changed, and all because of that tiny black spider.

While on a school field trip to the Hall of Science, Peter was accidentally bitten by the radioactive spider. Peter's teachers and classmates didn't see the glowing arachnid bite Peter, and they didn't see Peter rush outside to get some air.

Dazed, Peter wandered out into the middle of the street. He was only snapped back to reality when a taxicab horn honked at him. Peter knew that he had to react, so he closed his eyes and jumped.

When Peter opened his eyes again, he was clinging to the side of a building—three stories above the street! Peter couldn't believe it! Not only was he sticking to the wall, but he could climb straight up its side—just like a spider!

Aside from being able to climb up walls and ceilings, Peter soon discovered that he had super strength and that his reflexes were enhanced. He could move, think, and act faster than he ever had before!

Peter stood in an alley, awed by his newfound abilities. He realized that he must've gotten powers from the radioactive spider bite back at the Hall of Science.

Now that Peter had these amazing powers, he needed to put them to the test. He found the perfect opportunity to do so at a local wrestling match that night. He signed up to be in a match.

With a mask covering his face so that no one would recognize him, Peter stepped into the ring against a professional wrestler named "Crusher" Hogan. Crusher was the size of a gorilla and twice as strong, but he was no match for Peter Parker and his super spider strength!

Peter was paid well for defeating Crusher. He decided to use his new powers to earn some extra money. But first he would need a disguise. Using the spider as inspiration, Peter Parker created a new identity. He was now the amazing Spider-Man!

But Peter's costume was not complete. Peter created a special web fluid and web-shooters that let him shoot and swing from spiderwebs, just like a real spider.

One night while performing, a security guard yelled to Peter to help him stop a burglar who had stolen money from the wrestling arena. But Peter was only concerned with himself and did nothing to help the security guard or stop the thief.

Later, when Peter returned home, he saw police cars in front of his house. He rushed inside. Aunt May told him that someone had killed Uncle Ben. Just then, Peter overheard an officer say that the police had cornered the suspect down by the docks. Peter was enraged. He ran upstairs, changed into his Spider-Man costume, and swung off toward the docks.

Spider-Man crashed through the ceiling and landed in front of the criminal. The villain pulled out a gun, but Spider-Man shot a web at him and yanked the gun out of the criminal's hand. Then Spider-Man leaped into action and landed a powerful punch across the villain's jaw.

When the criminal's hat fell off, Peter was shocked to see that he was the same robber that he had let get away earlier in the night. If only Peter had not been so selfish! If only he had acted!

Peter used his webs to tie the criminal to a lamppost for the police to find. Then he remembered what Uncle Ben had always told him: “With great power comes great responsibility.” Peter finally understood what Uncle Ben had meant. He decided there and then to use his special powers for good. He vowed to always help those in need and to always fight for justice.

Peter Parker was no longer an average teenager. He was now a Super Hero. He had become the amazing Spider-Man!

MARVEL

PROFESSOR X

When Charles Xavier was a boy, he always listened when he heard other children talking about their dreams at night. They dreamed of winning soccer games or had dreams about being embarrassed. Charles's dreams were different. Charles knew he was not like other children.

In his dreams, Charles's mind would leave his body and go flying over his town. Charles could hear people's thoughts below. It turned out Charles was reading people's minds.

During his studies, Charles learned he was a mutant. He knew there had to be others like him. Charles traveled the world looking for mutants.

In Egypt, after a long day of searching, Charles went into a café. When he walked in the café, he could not relax because he felt something he'd never felt before — there was another mutant nearby!

Charles made eye contact with a large man in the room. He was really the mutant known as the Shadow King.

The Shadow King immediately recognized Charles as a mutant, too. The two mutants spoke in each other's minds.

"Join me, and together we can have all the power and wealth you can imagine!" the Shadow King said in Charles's mind.

"And spread fear and misery wherever we go?"

"The strong prey on the weak," said the Shadow King.

"No," Charles responded. "We must use our powers to help humanity, not enslave it!"

"Fool!" the Shadow King replied. "If you will not join me, then you must die!"

The Shadow King attacked with a fire-blazing whip, but Charles defeated him!

The second mutant Charles met was named Magnus. He had the power to move anything made of metal with his mind. Charles and Magnus became fast friends. But they did not always agree.

One day, Charles heard a commotion at a nearby hospital. Charles and Magnus found the evil Baron Wolfgang von Strucker launching an attack on a hospital.

"Stop!" Charles cried. "This is a hospital! They have suffered enough!"

"Stand aside!" Baron von Strucker said. "There's gold buried here! And it belongs to me!"

Together, Magnus and Charles took on the Baron! The Baron had many weapons, but between Magnus' ability to move metal and Charles's mental powers, they turned the Baron's weapons against him. Defeated, he ran away.

Charles and Magnus were successful, but the attack had changed them both. Magnus was convinced that humans were bad and not to be trusted. Magnus used his powers to steal the gold bars that Baron von Strucker had unearthed from the hospital.

"I shall use this wealth to fuel my plans to rule the world," Magnus said, "And some day, my friend, you will see that I am right and join me!" Charles just shook his head.

Magnus's plan made Charles think about his own future. His father had left him a mansion and a fortune. Maybe he could use this to help both mutants and humanity.

On his way home, Charles stumbled into a village where he sensed something was wrong. The minds of every person in the village were under a spell! Charles thought an evil mutant must be responsible. He searched the village, but did not find any.

He then discovered a hidden underground basement filled with strange machines. Charles knew these machines were being used to control the villagers' minds.

A frightening figure emerged from the shadows.

"What are you?" Charles asked.

"I am Lucifer. I am not from here," the alien said.

With an evil cackle, Lucifer pulled a handle as he fled from the room, releasing a giant stone from the ceiling of Lucifer's secret hideaway. Charles couldn't dodge it in time! The stone fell on him and he lost the use of his legs.

Instead of feeling sad about what he had lost, Charles thought about everything he needed to build.

Charles returned to the mansion where he had grown up. The house was dusty and empty, but it wouldn't stay that way for long. Charles got right to work creating the first part of his dream: a school for young mutants! He would name it Xavier's School for Gifted Youngsters.

MARVEL

DOCTOR STRANGE

Before he became a hero, Dr. Stephen Strange was anything but normal.

He was an expert surgeon at one of the largest hospitals in the country, with hands as skilled and precise as the tools he used to heal the wounded.

"Do you think you can fix him, Doctor?" one of the nurses asked.

"Of course I can fix him," an annoyed Stephen answered. "With these hands, I'm the best there is."

Being nice didn't matter to Dr. Strange. Being happy didn't matter. Making sure his patients felt comfort in times of need wasn't important. Stephen was a man who cared about one thing and one thing only—his work.

But very soon, Stephen Strange would begin to learn what truly mattered in life.

On his way home from the hospital one day, Stephen got into a terrible car accident.

The best surgeon in the city had found himself in need of saving by the very “friends” he had always been cold with. But every doctor’s first rule is “do no harm,” and that’s just what they did. They worked through the night, fighting to save Stephen’s life.

Days later, he woke, bones and muscles aching from surgery. Strange was refreshed, happy to be alive, and ready to get back to work. But, as his X-rays showed, that wasn't going to be as easy as he thought.

"The damage to your hands was too severe to repair," the surgeon admitted nervously.

"Cut to the chase," Strange demanded. "Will I ever hold a scalpel again?"

And with one simple word, Stephen Strange's life as a traditional doctor was over.

"No," the surgeon answered.

Stephen was desperate to get the use of his hands back. Without that, he felt his life was meaningless. But, time and again, doctor after doctor, specialist after specialist was as honest and cold with Strange as he had been with every patient he had ever cared for.

"There's nothing I can do," each said in turn.

One night, when Strange was nearly driven mad by sadness and despair, a mysterious voice woke him from his sleep.

"Do not give up, Stephen Strange!" the voice commanded. "You have yet to find the answers you seek."

"Who are you?!?" Strange demanded. "And how are you doing this?"

"If you wish for your life to have new meaning," the voice continued, "then simply follow the sound of my voice."

Over days, weeks, months, Strange traveled the world, listening to the voice echo in his head. Louder, louder it boomed, until finally. . .Stephen Strange found himself standing in deep snow at the bottom of a giant mountain.

With great effort, Strange toiled, troubled, and struggled his way up the mighty slope.

I haven't worked this hard since medical school, Strange thought.

"Then you are truly ready to begin your training," the voice answered. Except this time, much to Stephen's shock, the voice wasn't echoing inside of his head. . . it was coming from right in front of him!

The mysterious stranger introduced himself only as "the Ancient One." He explained that he had sensed Stephen's despair and loss from across the world. He offered to teach Stephen Strange the ways of the mystical arts so that he might become a new kind of doctor — one who didn't need a scalpel to heal the masses, but would use magic to save them.

"Magic is much, much more than simple parlor tricks," the Ancient One said. "It is the fabric that connects all things in the universe." The Ancient One coughed, with growing weariness, "I am getting older and need someone I trust to protect the world from those who would wish to hurt it."

A very angry man emerged from the shadows—his name was Mordo, the Ancient One's most senior student. "How dare you overlook your students and grant some stranger the power of Sorcerer Supreme!" Mordo growled.

The Ancient One calmly explained that he saw potential for greatness and compassion within the doctor, more so than any student he had ever instructed in the ways of magic. Furious, Mordo stormed away.

"This is preposterous! Magic won't do me much good in the operating room," Strange said. "If what you plan on teaching me can't fix my hands, then thanks—but no thanks!"

As Stephen left the Ancient One and his “preposterous” notion of magic behind, he couldn’t help but overhear something sinister.

Strange listened quietly as Mordo cast a spell, secretly whispering to a new, darker teacher—the wizard Dormammu!

“The Ancient One grows tired and refuses to teach me the secrets of the universe. Will you grant me the power to become the true Sorcerer Supreme?”

"No," Dormammu hissed, his voice flickering like a flame, "but I will grant you enough magic to defeat the Ancient One and claim his power for your own." Dormammu paused, then narrowed his eyes. "Once you've dealt with the one who would be our undoing!"

Stephen turned to run, but it was no use — magic, as they say, is faster than legs. Mordo cursed Stephen Strange with a dark enchantment — no matter how hard Stephen tried, he would never be able to speak or warn the Ancient One about Mordo.

As Mordo began to prepare for his assault on the Ancient One, Stephen Strange had to make a decision—would he leave and save himself or find some way to warn Mordo's target? Stephen realized he would have to fight Mordo, and in order to do that, he was going to need to learn something truly unbelievable.

Humbled, Strange returned to the Ancient One and asked if he might still be instructed in the mystical arts. Even though he couldn't reveal it to the Ancient One, Stephen knew that the only way to save the Ancient One's life was to fight Mordo's magic with magic of his own.

But the Ancient One saw into Strange's mind and knew the true reason for his change of heart. The Ancient One couldn't help but smile.

"You are not as selfish a man as you might think, Stephen Strange," the Ancient One said. "And that is why I grant you my power."

In an instant, Stephen was consumed by the power of the Sorcerer Supreme. It surged through Stephen's hands, and he knew while he would never be a surgeon again, he'd still be a doctor—and magic would now be his instruments. He felt connected to everything.

The entire cosmos—people, animals, Earth, sun, stars—was One.

And everyone needs a doctor from time to time.

With the help of the Ancient One, the hero repelled Mordo's attack, banishing him from the mountain temple. Though the battle was won, the war was far from over.

"Dormammu is a dangerous wizard," the Ancient One warned. "With Mordo as his pupil, they will attempt to attack again. And not just here. The entire world is in danger."

"Then we'd better hurry up with my training," Stephen said with a smile.

The Ancient One taught Stephen all the secrets of the mystic arts and soon, Doctor Strange found himself unlocking the secrets of the third eye and battling centuries-old dragons.

Now when Earth falls prey to threats supernatural, Stephen Strange is our first and last line of defense, a man feared by those who would wield dark magic. Doctor Strange is a practitioner of the mystical arts, the world's master magician. . .

. . .the Sorcerer Supreme!

MARVEL
BLACK WIDOW

Natasha Romanova wasn't always a super spy. Before she became the Black Widow, she and her little brother Alexi were orphans in Russia.

At a very early age, Natasha learned how to take care of herself and Alexi. She was very protective of Alexi. Natasha knew that they didn't have the advantages that other kids had, but she was going to make sure their life would be meaningful and good.

Natasha and Alexi lived in an orphanage called the Red Room. It wasn't like other orphanages. It was run by a man named Ivan, who trained the orphans to be spies. Natasha and her brother had intense training in martial arts. They had to learn to be very disciplined and know how to follow orders.

Natasha and Alexi took their studies very seriously. They worked tirelessly to become the strongest and challenged themselves every day.

Ivan was impressed with Natasha and Alexi. Everyone at the Red Room knew how hard this sister and brother had worked to stand out from the other orphans. They even battled two of the worst bullies at the Red Room. Natasha and Alexi's strength and wits won them the battle. Their hard work was rewarded. Everyone at the orphanage respected them.

Ivan asked Natasha to be the top spy. Natasha had a tough decision to make. She would have to leave her brother. Natasha remembered the promise that she had made to Alexi.

"Ivan, if you want me to be the top spy, you have to give me a partner," Natasha said.

"Nobody works with a partner. My spies work alone," Ivan replied coldly.

"If Alexi can't come with me, I'm going to have to refuse your offer," Natasha said. "I don't want to be top spy."

Ivan said, "I admire your dedication to your brother. I've never seen that before. You really care about him."

"He's my family."

Natasha and Alexi had many adventures. All the while, Alexi was in awe of his sister.

"You are like a black widow. So stealthy and powerful."

"I like that," Natasha said. The code name stuck.

But life wasn't easy, even though the duo was quite powerful. Natasha worried about her little brother. This wasn't the life she had imagined for him. Fighting criminals was a challenge. One evil villain chased them to a ledge of a very tall office building, and they had to use a rope to get down. No, this wasn't how she pictured Alexi's future. But she wanted to stick with him.

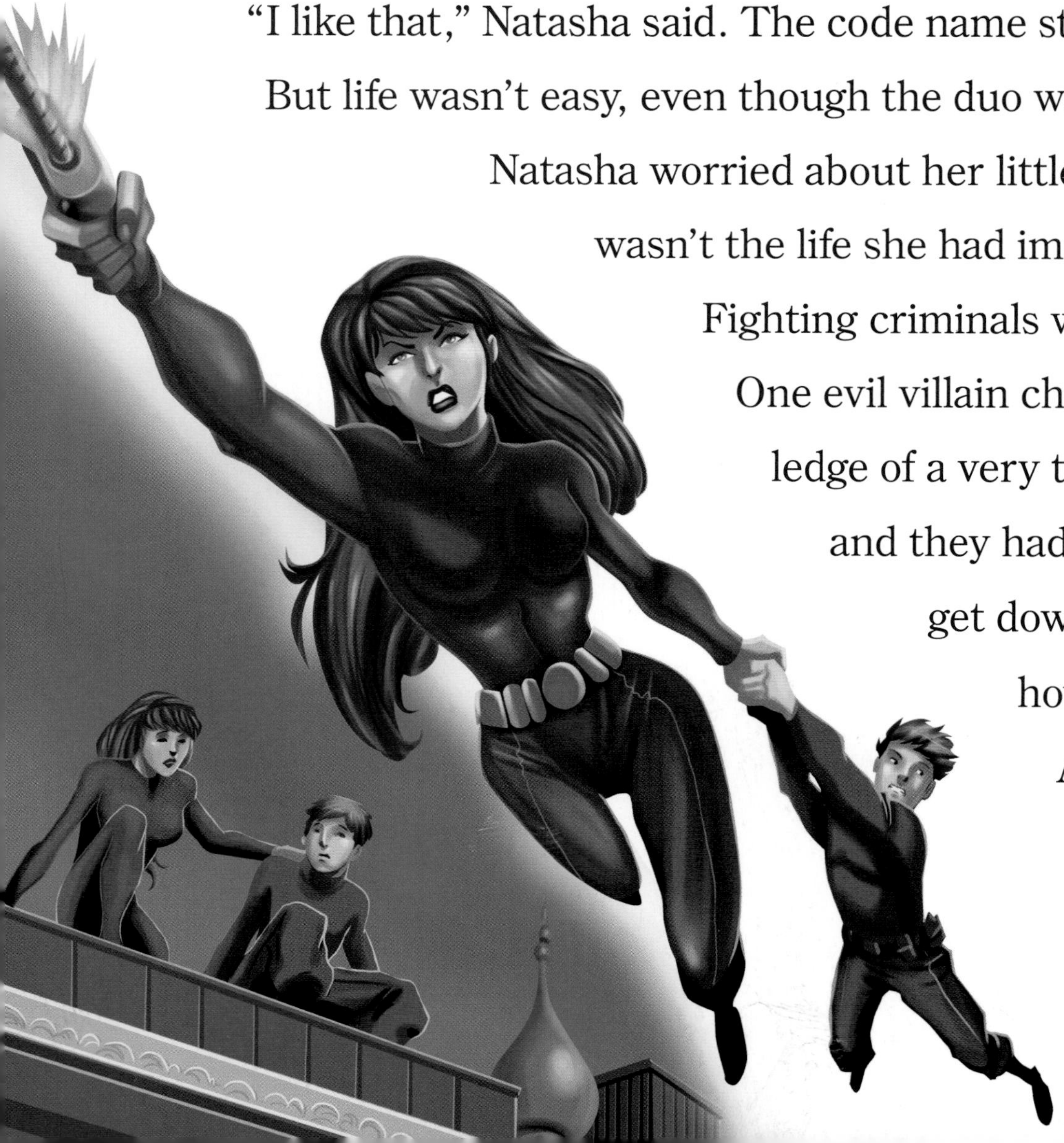

One day, Ivan called Natasha into his office.

"Alexi is too weak. I am going to erase his memory," Ivan told Natasha.

"No, you can't! I need him. He's my family!" she pleaded.

"It's too late. We already have him," Ivan said with a sinister smile.

Natasha tried to fight back, but she was outnumbered. She needed to find Alexi. If she could just get out of this office, she could save her brother! When it came to family, Natasha would do anything. She used her training to fight off Ivan's men and broke free.

Ivan stood up from his chair.

"There's no escaping, Ivan. You've trained me too well," Natasha said as she punched him.

"Natasha, stop!" Ivan screamed.

"It's not Natasha. It's the Black Widow, Ivan. Now give me back my brother!"

Ivan was helpless. He told her where he was hiding Alexi.

Natasha ran to Alexi. She cradled him in her arms.

"Alexi," she said, hopeful that his memory hadn't been erased.

Natasha knew everything was going to be all right now that her brother was safe. She would always try to protect him and others, because she would be the Black Widow.

MARVEL

ANT-MAN

Even in a world with scientists as brilliant as Reed Richards, Bruce Banner, and Tony Stark, Doctor Henry Pym stood out. Henry had loved science since he was a child, and after years of study, his knowledge of the field of biochemistry was amazing.

But many scientists found his work too complicated — they couldn't understand what Henry was trying to do. So they simply laughed at his idea of being able to shrink things.

"I'll show them," Henry said to himself. "Then we'll see who's laughing."

Henry worked day and night for months until he had his formula. Just a few drops of his serum would cause an object to shrink. Chairs, planes, anything could be shrunk down to the size of a doll's toy. A few drops from Henry's antidote would return the object to its normal size.

Henry was overjoyed. He'd done what the other scientists said was impossible. Now there was only one last step: testing it on a human.

It was the most dangerous step. So, naturally, Henry tested it on himself.

The serum worked — a little too well.

Henry found himself shrinking much faster than he had expected.

He looked up in dismay. He had placed the antidote on a window ledge, which was now much too high for him to reach.

Unsure of what to do, Henry stumbled outside. Maybe he could climb up to the window from out there.

Unfortunately, Henry wasn't alone outside.

A colony of ants noticed Henry. Thinking the scientist might make a tasty meal, the colony attacked.

Henry was able to dodge the ants for a little while, but he knew he wouldn't be able to keep it up for long.

He noticed one ant that wasn't attacking. Desperate, Henry jumped on the ant's back. To his surprise, the ant climbed up the wall.

Henry jumped off the ant's back and onto the window ledge. He pushed over the glass beaker holding the serum and climbed in. Immediately, Henry began to grow back to his normal size.

Henry decided his formula was far too dangerous and swore he'd never use it again.

But things didn't quite work out that way.

He was now fascinated by ants and studied the creatures tirelessly. He learned that ants are extremely strong for their size and can communicate with one another through a combination of sounds and smells.

Henry designed a helmet that would enable him to communicate with ants and a suit that would shrink as he shrunk.

Henry's research was interrupted by a request from the government. Henry was asked to invent a formula that would make people immune to radiation. It sounded impossible — so, of course, Henry was interested.

Before Henry was able to get very far with his formula, however, spies from another country broke into his laboratory. Henry wouldn't tell them anything, so they locked him up and made plans to blow up his lab — with him in it!

Henry was at the mercy of ruthless killers.

Or so they thought.

Although not a fighter by nature, Henry wasn't going to let his lab — or himself — be destroyed. If it's a fight they want, Henry thought, it's a fight they'll get.

Henry quickly donned the suit and helmet he'd created. Then he took the shrinking formula.

Ant-Man was born!

Using a rubber band as a slingshot, Henry sent himself flying through an open window.

Henry landed near the big anthill outside. This time, however, he wasn't afraid.

When an ant attacked, Ant-Man picked it up and threw it. "Even though the ant is now bigger than I am," Ant-Man realized, "I'm still as strong as I ever was as a full-grown man." Henry was excited to test to his new powers.

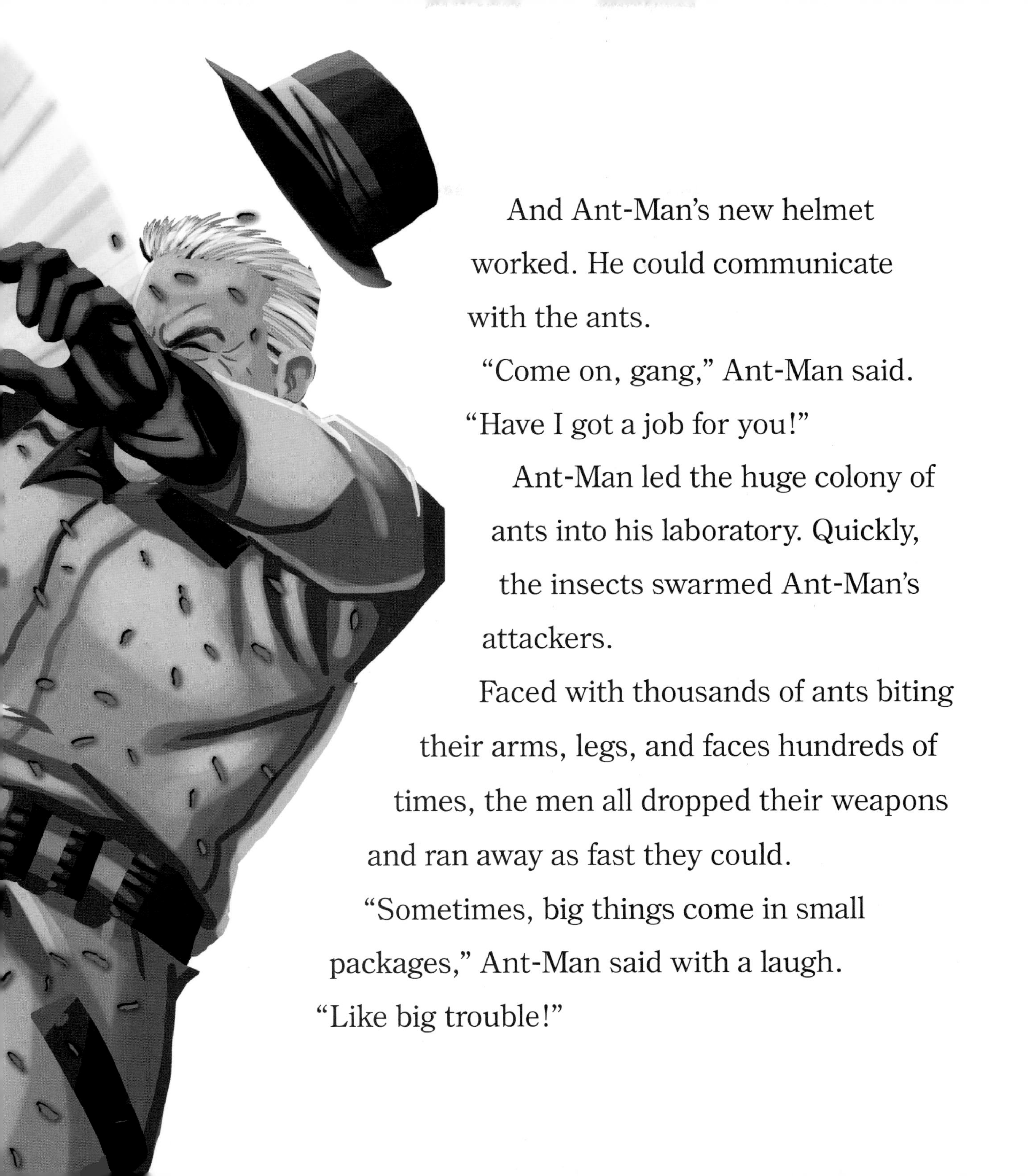

And Ant-Man's new helmet worked. He could communicate with the ants.

"Come on, gang," Ant-Man said. "Have I got a job for you!"

Ant-Man led the huge colony of ants into his laboratory. Quickly, the insects swarmed Ant-Man's attackers.

Faced with thousands of ants biting their arms, legs, and faces hundreds of times, the men all dropped their weapons and ran away as fast they could.

"Sometimes, big things come in small packages," Ant-Man said with a laugh. "Like big trouble!"

Henry decided that being a Super Hero was a good use of his time. He kept helping people, first as Ant-Man, later as Giant-Man, and soon after as a member of the Mighty Avengers.

MARVEL
CAPTAIN
AMERICA

No matter how much he ate or how often he exercised, Steve Rogers was always the smallest in his class. As a teenager, Steve, still small for his age, was willing to work hard for what he wanted — there was no one more dedicated. And what Steve wanted was to help. When America went to war, Steve knew what he had to do.

The next day, Steve went to an army recruiting station in New York City to enlist.

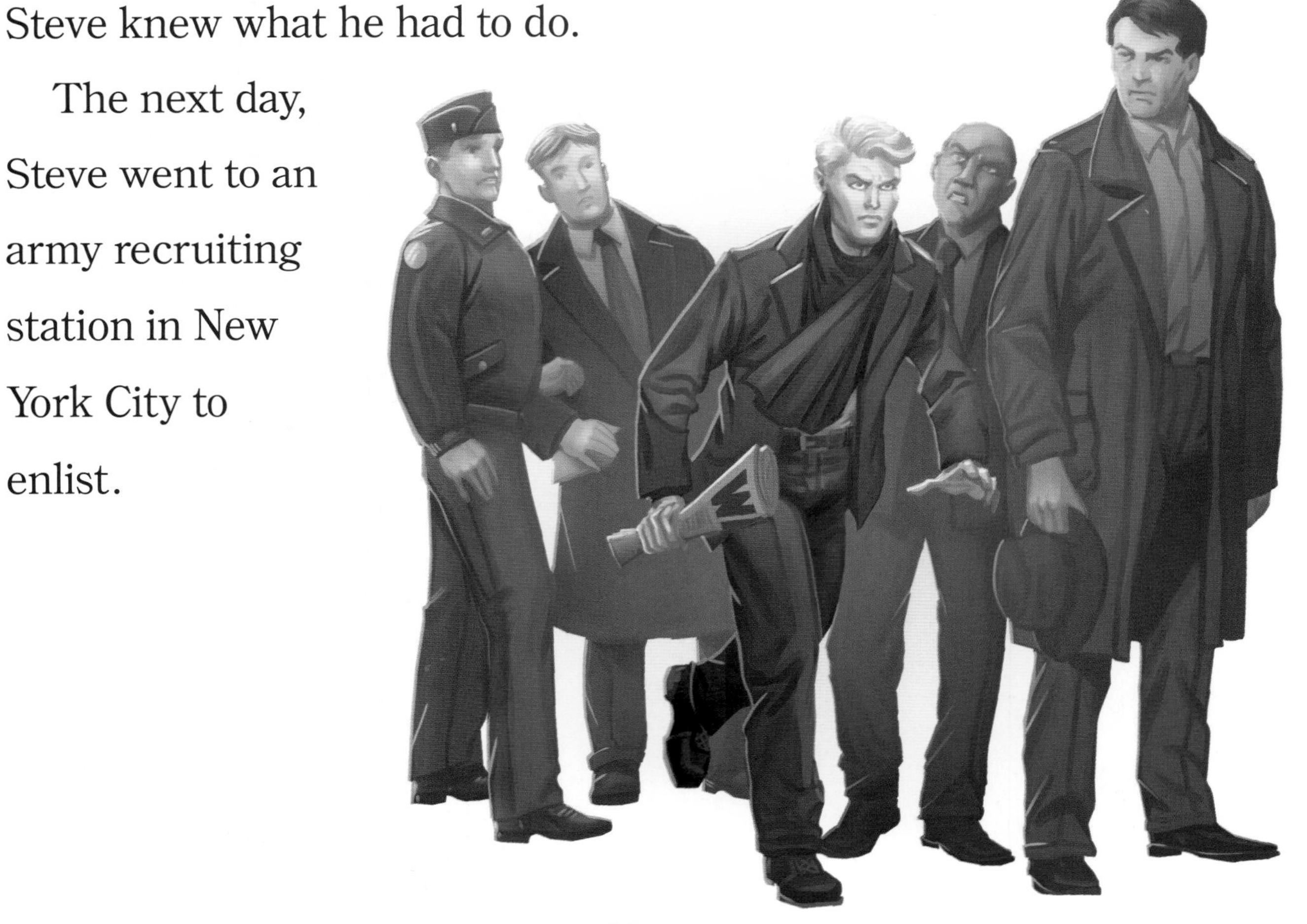

There were hundreds of other men there all lining up to join the army. Every man had passed so far, and Steve was confident he would, too. Steve was excited. But then a doctor led him into a separate room.

The doctor said, "We've run you through quite a few tests. Unfortunately, you're not fit to join the army."

Steve said, "I know I'm not very strong, but I'll do whatever I can to join the fight."

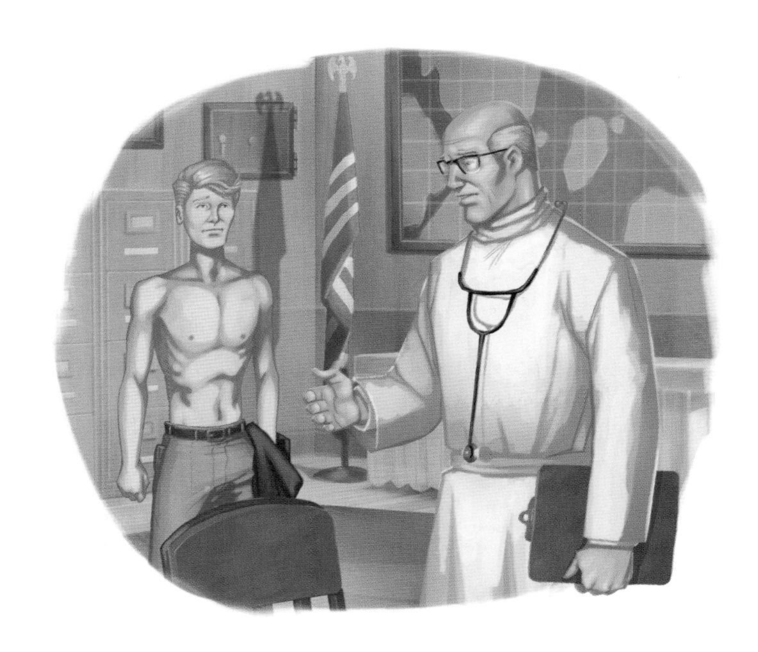

The doctor flashed a sudden smile. “Have you heard of Project: Rebirth?” he asked Steve.

The doctor called in General Chester Phillips, who was in charge of Project: Rebirth.

The general took Steve outside through a secret exit. A large car pulled up, and the two men got in the back.

They drove to a run-down antiques shop.

General Phillips went inside, and Steve followed.

"I believe you're expecting us," said General Phillips.

An old woman working there glared at the general.

"The watchword is, 'Rebirth shall occur this night,'" the general said quietly.

"Say no more," the woman said.

She pulled on a bookcase, and it swung away from the wall. There was a dark hole in the wall where the bookcase had been.

They went in and down some stairs to an underground lab. Steve watched in horror as the old woman grabbed the skin on her face and pulled. Steve realized she'd been wearing a disguise. She was not an old woman at all, but a secret agent!

General Phillips introduced Steve to the project's lead scientist, Dr. Abraham Erskine.

"We've been working on our Super Solider serum, and we're happy to finally test it," said Dr. Erskine.

Dr. Erskine stepped out of the room to complete the final step in the experiment: the Vita-Rays!

Bright blue lights turned on. They were so bright, Steve tried to shut his eyes. The rays were incredibly powerful. The room seemed to be spinning, and Steve felt a strange sensation. The rays were shooting into his body and transforming him.

Seconds later, Steve emerged from the experiment.

Everyone was staring at him. Confused, Steve looked down at himself—was he. . .was he bleeding? No, he didn't see any blood. No, he looked fine.

Steve glanced at Dr. Erskine for confirmation. The doctor's eyes were wide, and he was grinning.

Steve began to look his body over. His chest looked different. It was big and muscular, and so were his arms! He had huge muscles!

"We did it!" Dr. Erskine said with joy.

In the very next moment, the lab was attacked by a spy!

This enemy held up a small black grenade. He didn't want the Americans to have such great power! He threw the bomb.

Steve threw himself in front of Dr. Erskine before the bomb exploded.

But it was too late. Dr. Erskine was badly hurt and unable to duplicate the serum.

The army put Steve into a training camp right away. It was a special facility where he would learn how to use his new body.

General Phillips brought Steve into his office. He wanted to show Steve his new "uniform." The costume was necessary to keep Steve's real identity a secret. The general also had a special shield for Steve made of the strongest metal known to man.

Steve vowed to always fight for justice and what is right as the courageous Captain America!

MARVEL
DAREDEVIL

Daredevil. The man without fear. He may not be afraid of anything — but every criminal in New York City is terrified of him.

What these criminals don't know is that Daredevil is really just plain old Matt Murdock.

And although it's hard to believe, the daring acrobat who leaps from building to building high above the city streets . . . is blind!

Young Matt Murdock would have given just about anything to play ball like the other kids. But he couldn't.

"No games for you, Matt," his father said. "And never any fights. Promise me you'll be the best student in school."

"I will, Dad," Matt promised.

The other kids teased him. "There goes the daredevil himself," they would call. But Matt kept his promise.

He still dreamed of being a baseball player, though — or a boxer, like his father, "Battlin' Jack" Murdock.

One day, Matt saw an old man about to get hit by a truck. Without stopping to think about it, Matt ran into the street and pushed the old man to safety.

But Matt himself got hit. The truck was loaded with barrels of toxic waste. This poisonous substance splashed all over Matt, coating him from head to toe.

When Matt woke up in the hospital, he found he had lost the use of his eyes. He was blind.

But Matt found something else: all his other senses were much more powerful than before. He could hear people talking from blocks away. He could tell who people were by the smell of their perfume or shaving cream. He could read books just by feeling the ink.

Matt's new abilities gave him incredible control over his body. Soon, he was as skilled as an Olympic athlete.

But things weren't going so well for Matt's dad. He was getting too old—no one would let him box anymore.

Finally, in desperation, Matt's dad agreed to work with a man called the Fixer. He knew the Fixer wasn't a good man, but Matt's father needed a job badly.

At first, things seemed to be going well. Matt's dad was getting lots of work—and he was winning his boxing matches.

But one day, the Fixer told Matt's dad, "It's your turn now, Murdock. This time you lose. Understand?"

Matt's dad couldn't bring himself to pretend to lose. He won the fight — and the Fixer was not happy.

"Make sure 'Battlin' Jack' Murdock never fights again," the Fixer told his goons.

And he never did.

Matt felt that losing his father was even worse than losing his sight. And he was upset that the police were unable to find out what had happened to him.

He decided he would honor his father by keeping his promise: Matt went to law school. And once again, he was the best in his class. And he never fought.

After law school, Matt and his roommate, Foggy Nelson, opened up a law firm together.

But Matt couldn't stop thinking about his dad. He was determined to make sure justice was served. But how?

With his special senses, he could find anyone—and even beat them in a fight. But Matt had promised his father he would never act that way.

"Wait!" he said to himself. "*Matt* promised. But. . . what if it wasn't Matt Murdock doing the fighting? What if I became someone else? What if I used the name those kids used to tease me with? What if I became. . . 'Daredevil'?"

Daredevil's amazing senses enabled him to do just about anything.

By listening to someone's heartbeat, he could sense when that person was lying. He could track a man by the smell of his laundry detergent or tell how long ago a door had been opened by how warm the doorknob was.

And his senses combined to give him a sort of radar. Daredevil could leap off a building and know exactly how far away the nearest ledge, flagpole, or telephone wire was.

Daredevil decided he was ready to face his father's killer. He'd heard rumors that the Fixer was the man responsible for taking away his father—Matt's father. He knew that the Fixer could be found at a gym on the Lower East Side.

He decided the Fixer was going to get a surprise visit from a certain Super Hero.

When Daredevil entered the gym, everyone stopped and stared.

"Having trouble believing your eyes?" Daredevil asked. "Believe me, I know how that feels. I'm looking for the Fixer—I'm not concerned with the rest of you."

The men burst into laughter. "You *should* be worried about us, pal," the largest man said. "There are twelve of us and one of you."

"That doesn't seem like a fair fight," Daredevil said. "But I'll try to go easy on you guys."

Daredevil moved so quickly that none of the men could even get close. But he was able to get close to them — much closer than they liked.

Just then, the Fixer arrived. He didn't know who Daredevil was. But one look at Daredevil easily handling a dozen of his toughest guys told him he didn't *want* to know who Daredevil was!

The Fixer didn't make a sound—he just turned and ran. But no one was so quiet that Daredevil couldn't hear him.

Quick as a flash, Daredevil was after him.

Daredevil chased the Fixer down into the subway.

The Fixer was trapped—there was no escape.

"Who are you?" he gasped. "What do you want?"

"'Battlin' Jack' Murdock," Daredevil said. "Admit you were responsible for his fate!"

"Sure, I admit it. So what?" the Fixer laughed. "What good will that do you? Who's going to believe the word of a costumed freak?"

"No one." Daredevil smiled. "But they'll believe those cops behind you who heard the whole thing."

The Fixer turned to see a pair of police officers listening. The Fixer fainted from shock.

"What now?" Daredevil wondered. He'd done what he'd set out to do: he had gotten justice for his father.

"But there's a city full of people out there," he reasoned. "And a lot of them are in situations like mine. They need someone to help."

Daredevil grinned. "And whenever someone needs help, Daredevil will be there!"

MARVEL

WASP

When Dr. Henry Pym heard his doorbell ring, he had no idea his entire life was about to change.

"Hello, Dr. Pym," said the older man at the door. "I'm Dr. Vernon Van Dyne, and this is my daughter, Janet."

Henry had barely even noticed the man speaking to him. All he could see was the woman standing there. Henry thought she looked like an angel.

Dr. Van Dyne said he was trying to contact other planets. He hoped Henry's research could help.

"I'm sorry, doctor," Henry said. "I'm afraid I'm too busy, and my work is just too different."

Dr. Van Dyne was disappointed, but being a scientist himself, he understood. He and Janet returned to his lab, where he continued his experiments.

Unfortunately for Dr. Van Dyne, he succeeded.

Dr. Van Dyne barely had time to learn that not all alien creatures are friendly. Terribly upset, his daughter Janet called the one person she thought might understand what had happened—Henry Pym.

Henry agreed to send help: Ant-Man. He didn't tell Janet that he secretly *was* Ant-Man.

Ant-Man took one look at the wrecked lab and knew that Dr. Van Dyne's experiment had gone very wrong. His ant friends explained what had really happened.

Ant-Man brought Janet back to his own lab. "It was an alien that did it, wasn't it?" Ant-Man asked. "Which means there's a dangerous alien on the loose. We have to stop it before it hurts others."

Janet looked at Ant-Man. "Can you help me find the alien?"

"I think so," he said. "But I'll need help defeating it."

"I'll do whatever it takes," Janet said.

Ant-Man thought for a moment. Then he took off his helmet.

“Henry Pym?” Janet gasped. Then she nodded. “Your secret is safe with me,” she said, staring into his eyes. “What can I do to help? I’ll do anything.”

Henry injected Janet with the secret formula he invented. “This will enable you to shrink down to the size of a wasp,” he explained. “And you’ll be able to grow wings and antennae.”

“I assume,” Janet said, “that you’ve got a costume that will shrink along with me?”

"Oh!" Janet gasped as she tried shrinking for the first time. "I feel so strange!"

"You get used to it," Ant-Man said.

"What are we waiting for?" said the Wasp. "Let's go!"

Ant-Man's ant friends had located the alien. But even without their help, the alien wouldn't have been hard to find.

The army had been called out to fight the alien. And no wonder—it was now enormous. And the army's weapons had no effect.

"It's the size of a building!" the Wasp said.

"And look how powerful it is!" Ant-Man agreed. "What are we going to do?"

"This!" the Wasp said. She flew right at the monster. But her attack didn't work—she merely bounced off it.

"Wasp!" Ant-Man yelled, rushing toward her. "Are you okay?"

"I'm fine," the Wasp replied. "Just a bit bruised. That didn't go the way I planned. That thing seems unstoppable. And what's this stuff all over me?"

"That's odd," Ant-Man said. "It's some kind of acid on your costume where you touched the alien."

"Is the alien made of acid?" the Wasp asked. "And could you make an antidote to it?"

Ant-Man and Wasp raced back to the lab to get down to work. Soon, an antidote was ready.

"You *are* one of the world's greatest scientists," the Wasp said.

Henry blushed. "Now we need to find a way to get enough of this stuff on the alien—but as you discovered, we can't get too close ourselves."

"I think I know how," said the Wasp. "We'll just need to borrow some equipment from the army."

The army was more than happy to lend Ant-Man and the Wasp a tank.

"Here's hoping," Ant-Man said.

"Have a little faith," said the Wasp.

She was right. Their solution worked perfectly. As soon as the alien was hit by the antidote, it began to fade away.

"Nice work," the Wasp said to Ant-Man.

"I couldn't possibly have done it without you," Ant-Man replied. "We make a good team. How do you feel about continuing this partnership?"

The Wasp grinned. "I feel pretty good about it."

Not only would Wasp and Ant-Man become partners, they would also become members of Earth's mightiest mortals, the Avengers.

THE ORIGINAL X-MEN

Charles Xavier knew what it was like to be different. When he was a child, Charles lost all the hair on his head. Then he found out he was a mutant. Humans didn't like mutants. Finally, after a battle with an evil alien, Charles lost the ability to use his legs. But Charles Xavier did not let any of this stop him from fulfilling his dream.

You see, Charles had one goal in mind: to one day have humans and mutants living together peacefully. But Charles had many obstacles to overcome before his dream could come true. There were evil mutants, evil humans, and dangerous aliens that threatened the safety of the world. Charles would need help. That's why he created Xavier's School for Gifted Youngsters. He began recruiting other mutants from around the world to help him fight against these threats.

Xavier first met a young mutant by the name of Scott Summers. Scott could fire blasts of energy from his eyes. Charles decided to call him Cyclops!

The next mutant Charles recruited was scientist Hank McCoy. Hank was very smart and very athletic. He could run with his hands and swing with his feet. And so Beast was born!

The third mutant Xavier found was Bobby Drake. With the ability to turn into solid ice, Charles felt that the name Iceman best fit the teenager.

The group was growing. And their latest recruit was Warren Warthington III. Warren had feathered wings that helped him fly, so it was perfect to call him Angel!

Now that Charles had a class, it was time to help train them. Before long, they were controlling their special abilities and working as a team.

Charles welcomed Jean Grey, otherwise known as Marvel Girl, to the team. She had the power to move things with her mind!

The team was now complete. Charles Xavier, now called Professor X, decided he needed a special name for his band of mutant Super Heroes. All of his students had extraordinary powers that made them more than exceptional. And then Professor X smiled. Cyclops, Beast, Iceman, Angel, and Marvel Girl were now—the Uncanny X-Men!

The X-Men perfected their skills and abilities by training in the Danger Room. Every day, they got better and better at controlling their powers.

Soon, the X-Men were ready for their first mission. Professor X informed them that a mutant was attacking a nearby army base. But this was no ordinary mutant.

It was the professor's old friend, Magnus! He had taken his ability to control magnetic energy to become the villain known as Magneto. He would stop at nothing to defeat the humans and rule the world! But Professor X and his team weren't humans. They were the X-Men!

Cyclops led the charge against Magneto and unleashed his optical energy blast. But it couldn't break through Magneto's magnetic field.

Angel and Beast attacked the villain from the sky and ground, but it wasn't enough to take down the Master of Magnetism.

Using her telekinetic powers to launch missiles toward Magneto, Marvel Girl tried to defeat the villain. But Magneto proved too much for the young mutant.

Remembering their training in the Danger Room and what Professor X had taught them, the X-Men realized they needed to work as a team if they were going to have a fighting chance against Magneto. And that is exactly what they did! Cyclops with his optical blasts! Beast with his strength of a gorilla! Angel with his powerful wings! Iceman with his frost blast! Marvel Girl with her force field! The X-Men combined their great powers and began to drive Magneto back!

The X-Men had done it! They defeated Magneto and saved the army base! But the villain escaped, and the young team of mutants was very disappointed. The X-Men knew that this would not be the last time they saw the Master of Magnetism.

So the X-Men continued to train under the watchful eye of Professor X, who helped his students every step of the way to take control of their powers and abilities. And finally, after fighting many battles together, the X-Men graduated from Xavier's School for Gifted Youngsters and became full-fledged Super Heroes!

But their missions would not end with graduation. This growing family of friends continued to fight for Professor X and his dream of one day having humans and mutants live side by side in peace and harmony. They had to — they were the Original X-Men!

WOLVERINE

James didn't know he had special powers. He was just a kid growing up in the Canadian wilderness among the fierce wolverines. He never knew that he had something in common with that animal until one day, when he felt very scared and angry while trying to defend his family and his friend, Rose.

It was then that James's hands felt very strange. Without warning, James Howlett discovered he was something more than human.

Rose saw what was happening to James and knew people might see him as something threatening and scary. She grabbed him by the wrist, and they ran from the house.

They needed to go to a place where no one knew them and no one would hurt James. They arrived in a mining town, where they met a man named Smitty who was the head of a work site.

Smitty told James to remove his gloves—he wanted to see if his hands were good enough for working.

Rose was scared. She thought Smitty would see James's wounds from his claws, or worse—the claws themselves! But when James removed his gloves, there were no scars. Even though it seemed impossible, James had healed!

In order to keep their secret safe, Rose told the townspeople that James's name was Logan.

And as Logan grew up, he left behind his old life. He learned to be strong, stand up for himself and others, and always do what he knew was right.

He still had claws and was able to heal very easily. But he also learned he had an animal's senses — he could see, hear, taste, smell, and sense as well as a wild animal. Time continued to pass, but James didn't seem to age. His healing factor kept him young.

Eventually, he left the woods and began to travel the world. He fought in great wars. And during peacetime, he got married and settled in Japan. But then one day, upon returning home, Logan was kidnapped!

The people who took him hooked him up to a machine. They knew that his healing ability would help him survive their experiment. They erased his memory and coated his bones — and his claws — with an unbreakable metal called adamantium.

Logan managed to escape into the forest. He might have died if he hadn't been found by James and Heather Hudson. They nursed him back to health. But the only thing he could remember was his name — Logan.

James had been working for the government on a Super Hero project called Department H. He called himself Guardian. He thought Logan would make a good hero, too. He gave Logan a costume and a code name — The Wolverine! Together Guardian and Wolverine formed a Super Hero team called Alpha Flight.

Wolverine led Alpha Flight to victory in many battles. And even though he was proud of Alpha Flight and cared deeply for James and Heather, he didn't feel at home.

He still felt alone. He spent a lifetime searching for a family, and he finally found it. He joined a team of mutants. Like him, they were outcasts. Each was a loner. . . but together, they were a team called the X-Men.

He had been called many things—James, Logan, a Canadian hero, an X-Man—but the one thing that would never change, the one thing he would always be, was the unstoppable Wolverine!

FANTASTIC FOUR

Reed Richards loved science. It was his passion. He always won first place in the science fair at school, and at home he'd rather study mathematical formulas than play with other kids. He found the world of science and math fascinating. There was so much to learn, and Reed wanted to know everything.

Reed was rewarded for his knowledge of science. He even got to go to the state science fair. His teachers were proud of him. And, of course, if you read, study, and focus that well, you'll become an expert. And that's exactly what Reed grew up to be.

The more he learned, the more he realized just how much there was to learn. He was always reading about new scientific discoveries and dreaming that one day he would be a world-famous scientist.

Reed didn't lose his love for science as he grew older. He kept studying and loved it more than ever. By the time he was a teenager and most of his friends were starting high school, Reed was sought after by all of the country's best colleges and universities.

Since Reed studied a lot, he didn't have time for friends. When he found out that he was going to have a college roommate, he was very nervous. Not only was he awkward at making new friends, he had never had a roommate before. He wasn't sure how to act. His heart pounded as he opened the door to his new dorm room.

When Reed opened the door, he saw a big guy who didn't seem very friendly. Although his new roommate seemed intimidating, Reed also knew that he should keep an open mind.

"Hi, I'm Reed," he said, extending his hand.

Ben took it and smiled. "You must be the youngest kid on campus."

"Possibly," Reed said nervously.

"Well, I might be the biggest," Ben said with a laugh.

Reed realized that Ben wasn't what he appeared to be. He was a nice guy.

Reed and Ben became fast friends. They helped each other in class. In the evenings and on weekends, they would have meals together at the local diner. Reed loved cheering Ben on during his wrestling matches. They were always together. Reed learned how to be a good friend, and he enjoyed it.

In fact, Reed felt like he and Ben were such good friends that he shared something with him that he'd never shown anyone else.

They were Reed's plans for a new type of spacecraft. He had been working on it for years. This rocket wouldn't need fuel. It would use cosmic energy, like the sun's rays, to power itself. It wouldn't use up the Earth's air, water, or land. And best of all, it could be used over and over again!

"Wow, you have some fun ideas," Ben said as he looked at the diagram of the ship.

"Because it wouldn't use fuel, the ship could travel greater distances than humans have ever traveled before!" Reed gushed.

Reed really believed that he could make the ship. "I'm going to do it, Ben."

"Well, if you do, I'll pilot it."

The two roommates parted ways.

Even though he had been joking with Reed about piloting the spaceship, Ben joined the Marines after he graduated. And there he learned to fly planes and spacecraft.

Although they didn't live together, they kept in touch.

Reed continued his studies, all the while focusing on his perfect spaceship. He moved out of the dorm and into an apartment downtown.

Without Ben around, Reed was lonely. He became close friends with his landlord's niece, Sue Storm, and her younger brother, Johnny.

In fact, when Reed got the fantastic news that the government was going to help pay for his spacecraft project, he told Sue and Johnny even before he told Ben.

Reed spent the next few years building his ship. Reed's friends were very proud of him.

But before they could celebrate, the group was given some bad news. The government thought Reed's project had become too expensive, with no proof it would work. It was to be shut down immediately. Reed made a decision. He was going to test his ship before it could be destroyed.

Ben told Reed he couldn't do this without a pilot.

The ship worked! The flight into space was smooth and quick. But suddenly, the cabin went dark. The crew was thrown about, and they all began to feel strange. Johnny felt very hot. Ben felt so heavy, he couldn't move. Reed's head felt as if it would burst. And Sue felt sleepier than she ever had in her life.

Reed realized that the ship was about to crash. He struggled to turn on the autopilot. The ship rocketed to a rough but safe landing back on Earth. The crew escaped, and Reed figured that the ship must have been hit by a cosmic storm.

When they landed, Sue said that she felt very strange. And, suddenly, she seemed to disappear! She'd become invisible! But as quickly as it had happened, she reappeared. She called herself Invisible Woman.

Something had happened to Ben, too. Sue yelled out and called him a "thing"! It was the only way to describe what he'd become.

Reed had also changed. It seemed his body could bend into any shape imaginable. He called himself Mr. Fantastic.

Johnny would call himself the Human Torch because of his new abilities.

The group realized that Reed's experiment may not have worked the way he had wanted it to, but it had done something else incredible: it had given them fantastic powers. And they needed to use those powers to help mankind, just as Reed had intended to do with his spacecraft.

And from that moment on, the group of friends would be known as the amazing, incredible, awesome FANTASTIC FOUR!

MARVEL

THOR

In a land of myth and legend, a land far away from Earth, there once lived two brothers. They were princes of Asgard, a beautiful city among the stars where brave and worthy heroes walked.

The older brother, Thor, was loved by his people. Thor was mighty in battle. He fought great foes and won great victories against Asgard's enemies. Thor's younger brother, Loki, was known for his cleverness and mischief. Loki was a great sorcerer and, although his magic was not as respected as Thor's great strength, together the brothers kept Asgard safe.

One day, their father, King Odin, took Thor aside and showed him a mighty hammer. "This is Mjolnir," Odin said. "I had it made just for you."

Eagerly, Thor tried to pick up the hammer. But Mjolnir did not move.

"Only one who is worthy can lift the hammer," Odin said.

"But am I not worthy? I have won many great battles," Thor said.

"There is more to being worthy than battle," Odin replied.

But Thor did not understand. Again and again, day after day, he tried to lift Mjolnir. Loki, jealous of his father's attention to Thor, smiled smugly at his older brother's failure.

Frustrated that he couldn't lift the hammer, Thor turned to his brother. "Loki, come with me, brother! Let us find a battle where I can prove myself!"

"Of course. I would be honored to serve the great and mighty Thor," Loki replied. Thor did not notice his brother's sneer.

Just then, a servant of Asgard ran into the room. "The Giants of Jotunheim attack, your royal highnesses!" This was an opportunity for Thor to prove himself!

Quickly, Thor and Loki traveled to Jotunheim. For days, the brothers fought side by side. Thor was like a whirlwind. His great sword clashed against his enemies. Loki attacked with all the strength of his magic and the cunning of his mind.

Together, the brothers fought back the Giants of Jotunheim until none stood in their way. They defeated the Giants and were going to return to Asgard as heroes. Thor and Loki were pleased.

When the brothers returned, all of Asgard threw them a victory parade. Thor and Loki had saved them yet again. But Thor didn't pay attention to the cheering crowds. Ignoring his father's open arms, Thor quickly rushed to the room where Mjolnir lay. Surely now the hammer would find him worthy!

But even though he pulled with all of his great strength, Thor could not move the hammer.

"You still do not understand," Odin said.

But Thor was not ready to give up so easily. He gathered together other great fighters of Asgard—the brave warrior Balder, the strong and beautiful Lady Sif, and a band of soldiers called the Warriors Three.

As he spent time with these loyal companions, Thor thought less about the room with the great hammer in it. Thor didn't think about the glory he would win with Mjolnir. He thought about all the good he could do for Asgard.

Odin watched Thor with growing pride. One day, Odin led his son back to the room where Mjolnir lay. "It is time."

With a powerful heave, Thor lifted Mjolnir. He had done it!

However, this moment of greatness did not last. Now that he had the mighty hammer, Thor began to ignore his loyal companions and once again think only of himself. Odin sadly watched as his favorite son let the power of Mjolnir go to his head.

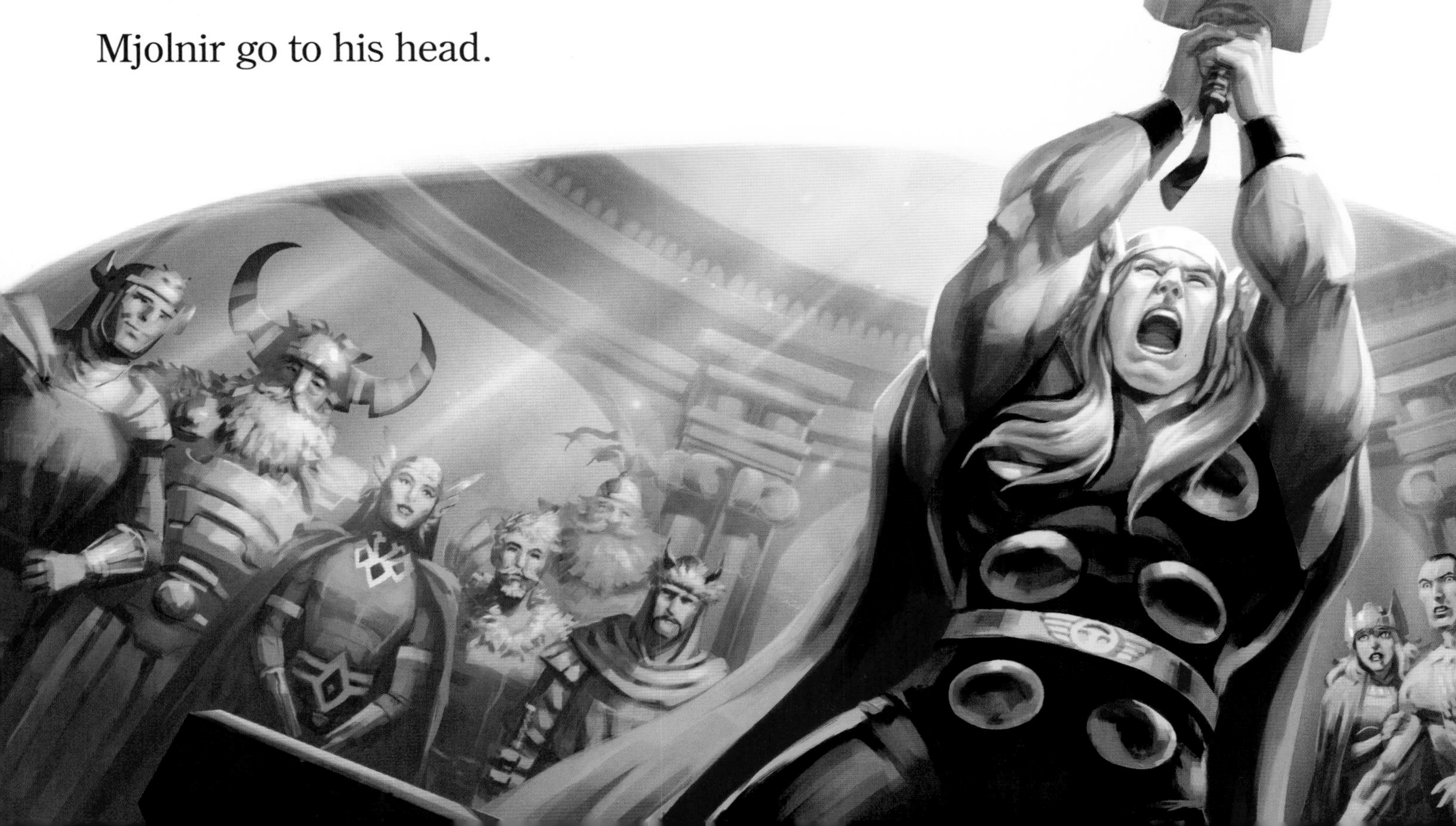

One day, Odin called Thor to his throne room.

"You are the bravest warrior in Asgard, Thor. But there is no honor in your actions," Odin told Thor angrily. "You do not know humility. You do not understand what it is like to be weak or feel pain. Because of your arrogance, I banish you from Asgard and take back my gift of the mighty Mjolnir."

Odin sent Thor across Bifrost, the rainbow bridge, to the distant planet Midgard—the planet we call Earth. Odin also took away Thor's memory. Thor believed that he was a doctor with an injured leg named Don Blake. As Blake, Thor had to work hard and care for others.

Years passed, and he began to let other people to help him with his injured leg. As a weak human, Thor learned what he had never understood as a mighty warrior—a true hero fights not to win glory, but to help and protect others.

Watching from Asgard, Odin saw that his son had learned compassion. Despite Loki's disapproval, Odin decided to bring Thor home.

Don Blake felt a strange urge to travel to Norway and to a particular mountain. Here, he discovered a stick that was much more than it appeared. It was Mjolnir in disguise! Don Blake raised the mighty hammer and became who he had always been: Thor, Prince of Asgard.

Thor was welcomed back to Asgard by his faithful friends and his loving father. Loki, however, was not pleased to see his brother. While Thor's time away from Asgard had made him wise and kind, his absence had made Loki more wicked and selfish. Loki had hoped that without Thor, he might become the next king of Asgard. In anger, Loki stormed out of his father's throne room and vowed revenge.

Thor was sad to see Loki go, but he promised himself that one day, they would be brothers again. But for now, he alone would be a mighty guardian. He would protect both of his worlds — Asgard, where he had learned to be a warrior, and Earth, where he had learned to be a true hero.

MARVEL

SHE-HULK

When Jennifer Walters was a girl, she loved dolls and playing dress-up. But she loved other things, too — things that boys usually liked. Things like baseball.

"Don't be stupid! Girls can't play baseball!" the boys would say.

Eventually, she stopped trying to join them.

Boys didn't like it when Jen tried to play their games. And girls didn't like the fact that Jen wanted to play with the boys. As she grew older, Jen became shy and quiet. She thought that if people got to know her, they wouldn't like her very much.

So she mostly kept to herself.

The one person Jen could be herself around was her cousin, Bruce. Like Jen, Bruce was a quiet kid who kept to himself. Bruce was a few years older than Jen, but the two of them were the closest of friends. And when they were together, they had nothing but fun.

No matter how quiet Jen was, she was always ready to stand up for her favorite cousin in the world. Bruce would do the same for Jen. They protected each other.

Bruce was the kind of kid others would pick on. But Jen, though quiet, was the type to never allow a wrong to go unpunished.

"You leave my cousin alone!" she often found herself saying to kids twice her size.

"Yeah, who's going to make me?" was usually the reply.

"Stick around, and you'll find out!" Jen would answer. And she always found that the bullies would back off.

"Dumb girl!" they'd usually say as they stomped away.

"You're going to get yourself hurt one day if you keep on talking to bullies like that!" Bruce told her.

Jen shrugged. "Maybe," she said, "but at least I'll know I tried."

"Tried what?" Bruce asked.

"To stand up for myself, silly. And for any other innocent kid who's getting picked on!"

Bruce smiled and shook his head.

"I still think you're crazy," he said, laughing.

But Jen wasn't dumb or crazy. She was smart and focused, and as she grew older, she knew she wanted to fight for others as a lawyer. Even though everyone told her that she was a silly dreamer, Jen studied hard and earned her degree.

"I'm so proud of you, cuz," Bruce said as he hugged Jen at her graduation.

"Not as proud as I am of you, Doc," Jen said to Bruce, who had recently become a doctor of science studying gamma radiation.

Bruce's job was so dangerous that an accident had caused him to change into a big, green, powerful but uncontrollable hero called the Hulk any time he was upset.

But Jen's job was dangerous, too. She spent her days arguing to put criminals behind bars. And one of these criminals was not very happy about it.

One night, while Bruce was visiting Jen, the crook hid in the shadows and hurt Jen.

Bruce opened his medical bag and took out his instruments to help her.

There was only one thing he could do, and only one way to save Jen. Bruce needed to use his skills as a doctor. He knew from when they were kids that he and Jen had the same blood type. He would give her his own blood to replace what she'd lost.

Bruce's plan worked. When Jen woke up, she'd found that Bruce had made sure she was safe in a hospital room.

But she wasn't as safe as Bruce had hoped. The crook who'd tried to hurt Jen had pretended to be a doctor and found his way to her room.

The crook planned to finish her off for good! Jen recognized him and immediately felt threatened. Suddenly, she felt a rush of blood to her head. And then, something happened. . . .

Jen felt more powerful than she ever had before. She knew right away that Bruce's blood had affected her strangely. Whatever had changed him in that gamma-ray accident must have been transferred to her own body through his blood. She'd become a Hulk!

Or, as the criminal said, "You're. . . a . . . a SHE-HULK!"

Jen smirked. She kind of liked the sound of that!

Jen heard sirens outside the hospital room. She smashed through the wall to get to them quickly and hand over the criminal.

"Here you go, officers. I found this man wandering around the hospital, pretending to be a doctor and trying to hurt a patient," Jen said. "You'll want to lock him up so he won't hurt anyone else."

"That's Nick Trask!" an officer said. "He's the most wanted man in Los Angeles!"

"Th-Thank you, ma'am," another officer said. "But . . . who are you?"

"Just call me what *he* called me," Jen said. "CALL ME SHE-HULK!"

MARVEL
HAWKEYE

Clint Barton and his brother Barney grew up in an orphanage. One of their favorite things to do was make up stories about being Super Heroes. They'd spend hours at the playground wearing capes and masks, pretending to save the world from villains.

When they were older, the boys left the orphanage and were so excited to see the world. One evening, the boys came across a large tent.

"What's this?" Barney asked his brother.

"It looks like a circus tent," Clint said. "Remember when we read that story about the traveling circus? Now we can really see what it's like! Let's peek in."

"Wow!" Barney gasped when he saw the trapeze artists high above the audience. "This is so cool! Maybe we could work here."

The brothers were thrilled to get jobs with the circus.

Clint was incredible with a bow and arrow. When the circus folk saw how talented Clint was at archery, he became a headlining act. He was known as Hawkeye, the World's Greatest Marksman. He was the star performer, and people traveled to see him. The circus became very successful and made lots of money.

One night after a sold-out show, Hawkeye saw the light on in the box office. He was shocked to see another performer, the Swordsman, stealing money from the cash box.

"What are you doing?" asked Hawkeye.

The Swordsman pushed Hawkeye and ran off. Hawkeye aimed his arrow at the Swordsman but couldn't bring himself to hurt him. The Swordsman had been Hawkeye's mentor.

The other people in the circus felt differently. They were upset that Hawkeye didn't stop the Swordsman. They asked him to leave the circus.

Hawkeye started performing his act at a beachfront carnival. One day, there was an explosion on the Ferris wheel. People were stuck on it and in danger of falling off. He wanted to help.

As he looked up at the sky, he saw a red and gold streak. It was the invincible Iron Man. The Mighty Avenger lowered the damaged ride to safety.

Hawkeye was in awe of this hero. Just as Hawkeye dreamed when he was a little boy, he wanted to be a Super Hero. He wanted to be like Iron Man.

Inspired by Iron Man's rescue at the Ferris wheel, Hawkeye went home and made a costume of his own. He also created a variety of special arrows.

"I'm not just Hawkeye the performer," he said aloud as he sewed the last stitches on his costume. "I'm Hawkeye the Super Hero."

Hawkeye put on his new costume. Later, he saw someone robbing the local jewelry store. The thief took one look at Hawkeye, dropped the loot, and ran away. When Hawkeye picked up the bag, the police thought he was a criminal.

Just then, Iron Man came down to serve justice. Hawkeye tried to explain that he was innocent, but Iron Man didn't believe him and blasted his repulsor ray.

Hawkeye attempted to defend himself with his bow and arrow. He trapped Iron Man in a net.

"I'm not a jewel thief. I want to be a Super Hero like you," Hawkeye told Iron Man.

The Avengers came to Iron Man's rescue.

Iron Man announced, "Don't hurt this man. He is innocent. I just heard over my armor's radio that the police have caught the real thief."

The Avengers were impressed with Hawkeye.

Hawkeye helped Iron Man out of the net. They shook hands.

"You did a great job today," Iron Man said. "I want you to meet the Avengers. I think you'd make a great addition to our team."

Hawkeye's childhood dream had come true. He was a Super Hero!

MARVEL

SPIDER-WOMAN

Jessica Drew's parents were on to something big!

Both her mother and father were doctors. And both specialized in the study of spiders.

They knew spiders and their relatives had lived longer than most creatures on Earth.

They knew that spiders were powerful, quick, and dangerous.

They knew that if they could somehow capture a spider's power and give it to someone, that person might live a very long, healthy life.

They also knew that their research was so specialized and sensitive that they needed to locate their lab in a very secret place. They chose the hills and valleys of a place called Wundagore.

But for all the things the doctors knew, there was one terrible thing of which they were unaware.

Their lab was built upon natural stores of radioactive elements. And radiation can hurt people if it's not carefully controlled.

By the time she was ten, Jessica was feeling very sick from all the radiation around her.

Her parents knew that there was only one thing that might save their daughter. They knew from their tests that spiders could survive uncontrolled radiation much better than humans. So they used a special ray they had invented to get the spider's DNA into Jessica.

But the doctors soon learned that the treatment had made her far stronger than they had anticipated. Soon, Jessica's fingers were sticking to surfaces. She was able to leap and jump farther than anyone would have thought possible. And, over time, she learned that she could shoot power straight from her hands!

The treatment had turned Jessica into something more than human and more than spider, making her a little bit of both! And as she grew older and learned how to use these fantastic powers, she began to call herself something to reflect that combination. She began to call herself. . .

Spider-Woman!

And as Spider-Woman, Jessica dedicated her life to fighting crime.

Her adventures took her all over the world, and even outside of it, to distant planets. She was always ready to use her powers to battle evil wherever it might be found, in whatever form. From petty criminals to Earth-conquering aliens, Spider-Woman was always there to save the day!

And time and time again, Jessica proved that a Spider-Woman was just as good as any Spider-Man.

SILVER SURFER

The Silver Surfer is an intergalactic Super Hero. Villains fear his power, but he would give it up for the chance to return to home.

Years ago, he was a scientist named Norrin, happily living on the peaceful planet Zenn-La. One day, he made an amazing discovery.

Norrin was the first of his people to discover a massive object heading toward Zenn-La. He was looking forward to making contact with an alien race.

The alien visitor was Galactus, a powerful and gigantic alien who traveled the universe looking for food.

And food to Galactus was planets! No one had any idea how to stop Galactus. And now he had come for Zenn-La.

Norrin hoped he could communicate with Galactus. He went in a spacecraft toward him.

A deep voice echoed off every surface of Norrin's ship: "I am Galactus, devourer of worlds! Who dares approach?"

"I am Norrin Radd, of the planet Zenn-La," said Norrin. "Please, spare my people! We are a peaceful world, and we've done nothing to anger you."

"I will spare your wretched planet, but there is a price," said Galactus. Galactus raised his arm and fired a beam of energy into Norrin's ship.

"I will leave your people in peace if you become my herald. You will find planets that have a strong enough life force to sustain me. If you fail, I will return for your planet!"

The power that fueled Galactus was known as the Power Cosmic, and Galactus transferred some of it to Norrin.

Norrin was transformed! His skin was coated with a silvery metal that protected him from harm, and he was filled with a never-ending and amazing power. He was sad to leave the only home he had known, but he knew that it was the only way to protect his planet.

"Good-bye, my friends," said Norrin. "I may never see you again, but please be well."

"Norrin!" pleaded his mother. "Please be kind to other people! Thank you for saving us, but don't let Galactus destroy other people's homes."

For years, the Silver Surfer acted as Galactus's herald. He sought out planets that did not have any intelligent beings. He was able to follow Galactus's wishes without harming others.

With time, Norrin began to enjoy his travels. From multicolored stars to planets made of icy volcanoes to worlds with endless rivers of lava, he saw the majesty of the universe. The scientist in him never tired of finding new things.

Then one day, he discovered the planet Earth.

As Norrin approached Earth, a scientist and Super Hero named Reed Richards realized that his planet was about to be visited by aliens. Reed Richards was also known as the super-elastic Mr. Fantastic, the leader of the Fantastic Four!

"I don't know what's going on yet, but we should check it out," Mr. Fantastic said to the rest of his team.

"I am sorry, but your world is about to face the wrath of Galactus," said the Silver Surfer.

"We ain't letting a giant spaceman eat our planet," growled the Thing. "It's clobberin' time!" But the Silver Surfer's powers were too much for the Super Heroes to handle.

The valiant efforts of the Fantastic Four reminded Norrin of his own efforts to stop Galactus. He couldn't let Galactus destroy the Earth any more than he could let him tear Zenn-La apart!

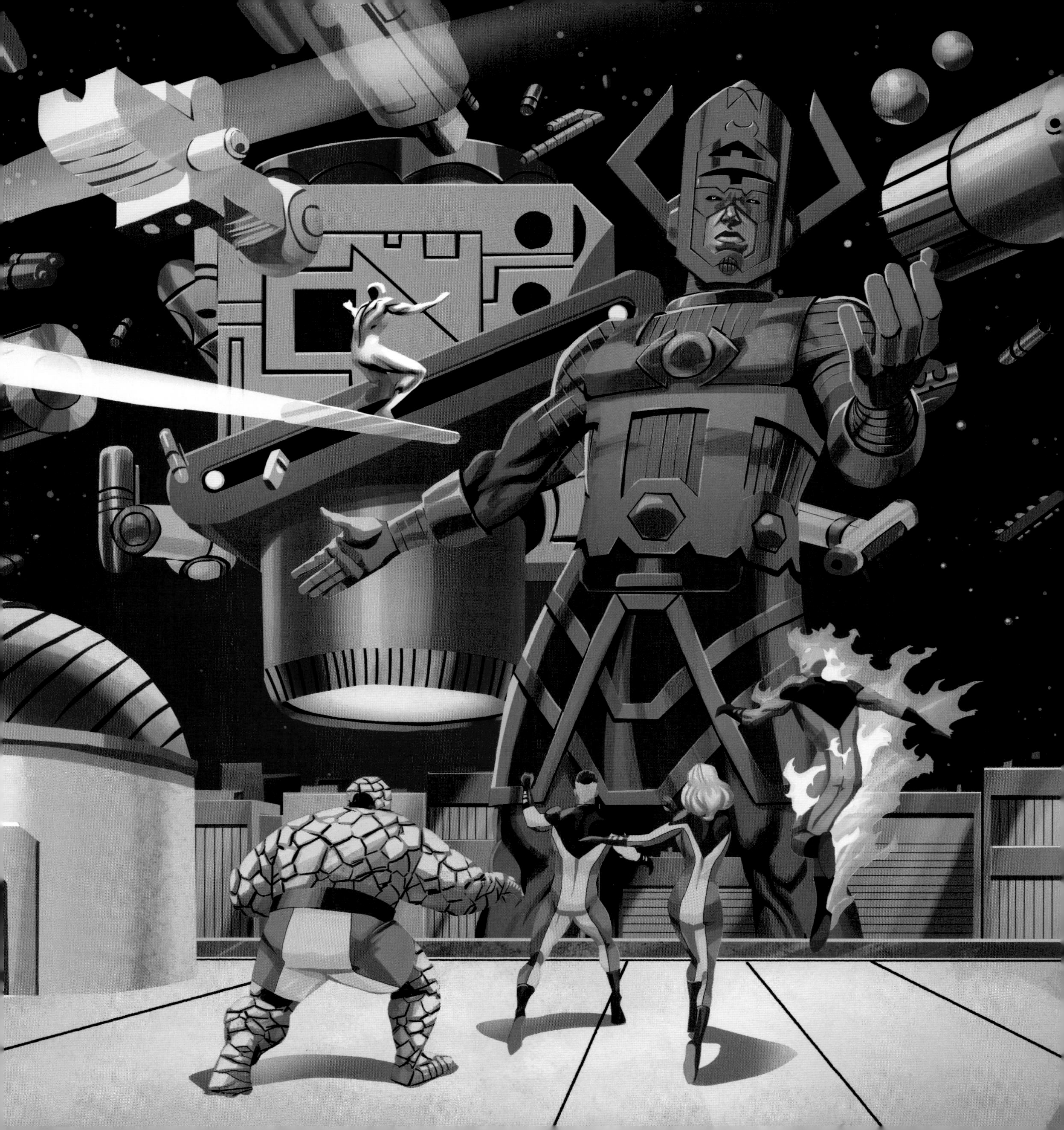

"Mighty Galactus!" shouted the Silver Surfer. "There must be another way!"

Galactus's voice boomed, "There is no other way! Do not fight me! I gave you your powers, and they will have no effect on me. This planet will be mine, and then you will find me another. And another. Or your precious Zenn-La will pay the price!"

But even the combined might of the Silver Surfer and the Fantastic Four couldn't stop Galactus! The machine that Galactus used to devour worlds was now complete.

Just when it seemed like all hope was lost, Reed's brilliant scientific mind began to form a new plan. He needed to create a device of his own — one that could harness the incredible cosmic power of the Silver Surfer.

"Your power comes from this 'Galactus' creature?" asked Mr. Fantastic.

"Yes," replied the Silver Surfer. "But my power has no effect on it."

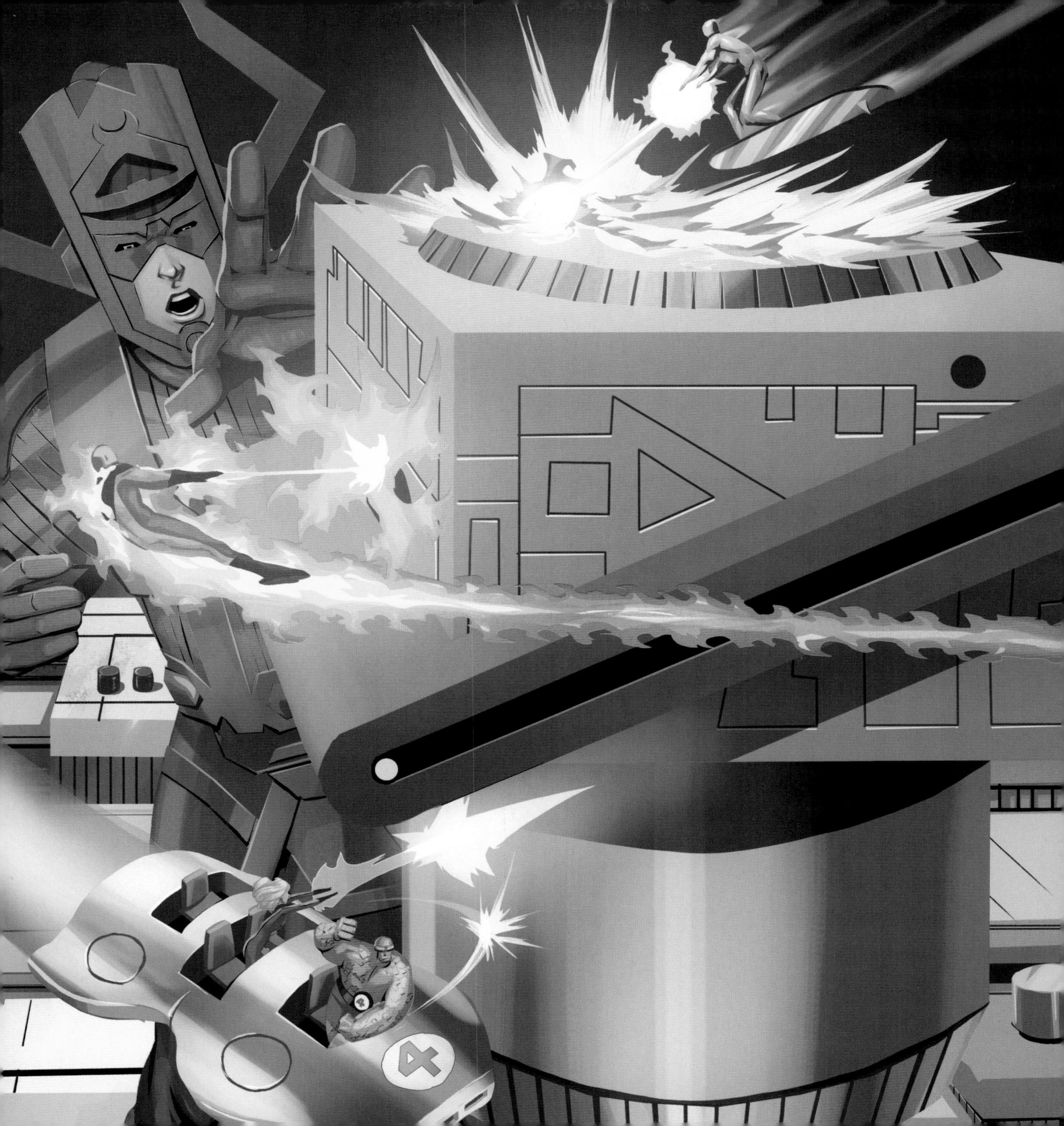

"Never say never, my friend," said Mr. Fantastic. "I have an idea! I need to get to my lab!"

The Silver Surfer fired into Reed's device, which then hit Galactus. Galactus was knocked backward by the blow, and he was glowing from head to toe.

"What. . .what have you done, human?" Galactus demanded.

"I redistributed your power to be in alignment with the energy you would get from consuming our planet," said Mr. Fantastic. "In short, just as the Silver Surfer's power alone has no effect on you, your powers will no longer have any effect on the Earth. It's called the Nullifier, and I'd say it's working as planned."

“Maybe you should try eating a planet that isn’t full of living beings,” the Invisible Woman added.

“Norrin!” Galactus boomed. “Your betrayal may have won the day, but it has also sealed your planet’s fate!” With that, Galactus and his machine floated up through the air and back into space.

“We did it!” the Silver Surfer exclaimed. The Earth was saved! But Mr. Fantastic knew they still had work to do.

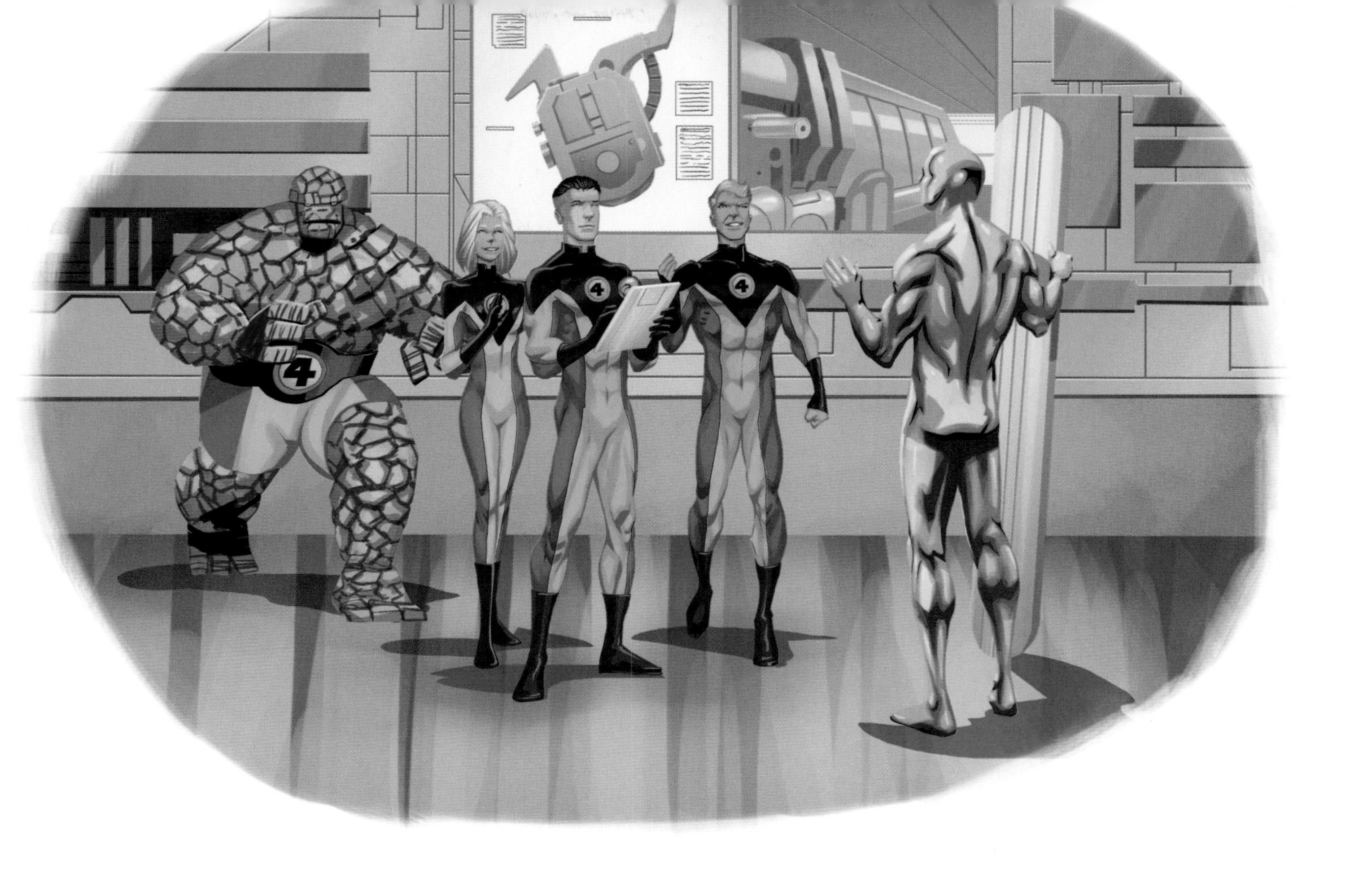

The Fantastic Four knew that the Silver Surfer had risked not only his life, but the life of everyone on his home planet of Zenn-La by betraying Galactus.

Working together, the Silver Surfer and Mr. Fantastic combined their skills and were able to send a message to Zenn-La. They sent the instructions for the creation of the Nullifier!

But there was something keeping the Silver Surfer trapped on Earth. Galactus wasn't able to take the Power Cosmic back from Norrin, but he had figured out how to keep the Surfer on Earth.

The Silver Surfer would always have his powers, but that meant he wouldn't be able to go home. Devastated, he returned to the Fantastic Four's headquarters.

"I promise, we will try to find a way for you to break Galactus's barrier," said the Invisible Woman.

"And hey, if you're going to be here for a while longer, you should enjoy yourself," said the Human Torch. "The Earth's a pretty cool place! You should go get a burger. Hey, do you even eat?"

Mr. Fantastic invited the Silver Surfer to stay with them at the Baxter Building.

After exploring the ends of space by himself for so long, the Silver Surfer was happy to once again live among other people. Like his friends in the Fantastic Four, he spent his days helping people and exploring new places.

He knew that he would never stop trying to find a way to return home to Zenn-La. But he was also at peace, finally in control of his own life. The Silver Surfer had truly found a new home, and he was now the Earth's first intergalactic defender!

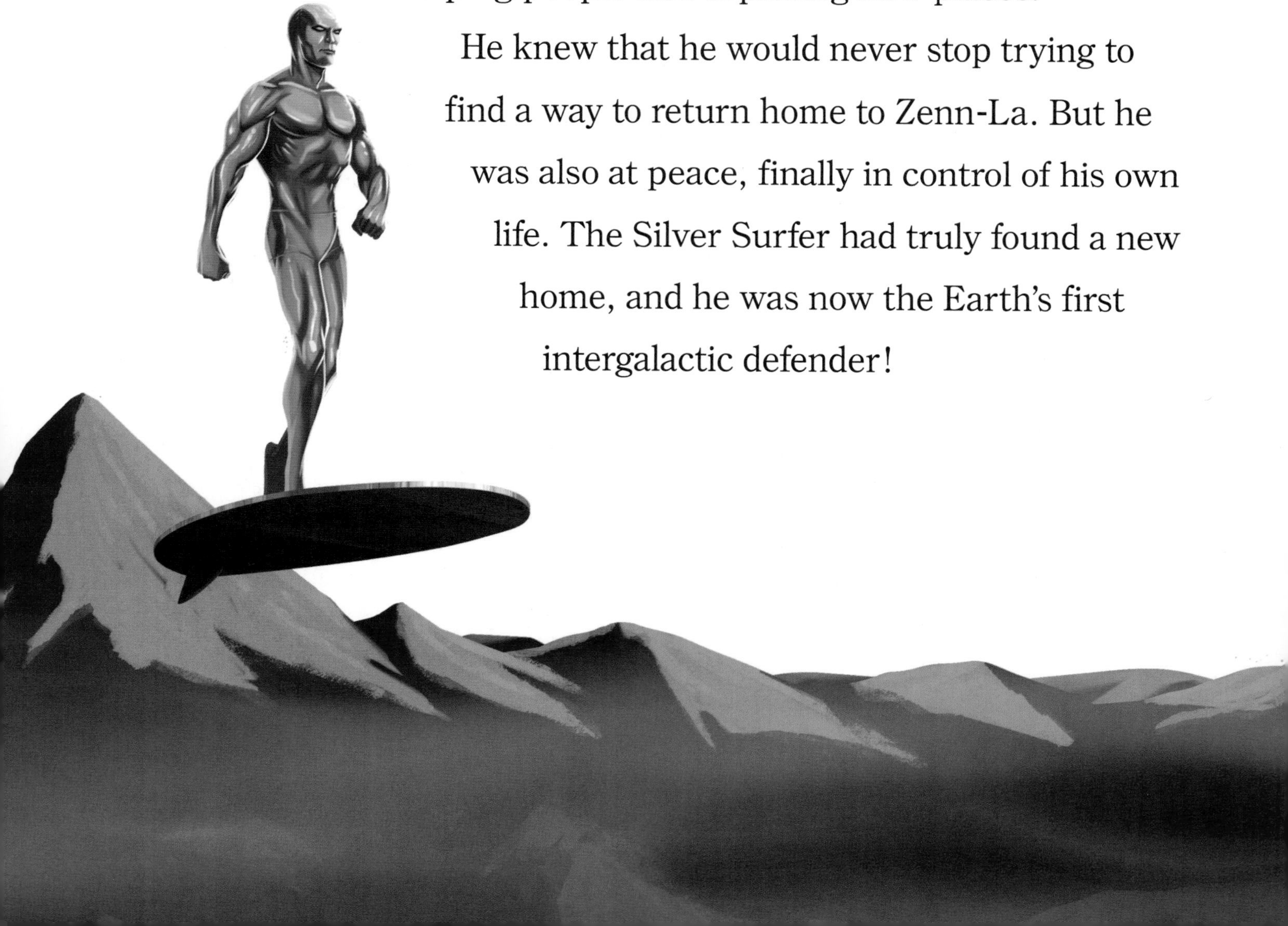

ALL-NEW X-MEN

The X-Men were a special kind of Super Hero team. They were mutants—heroes born with special abilities. Professor X, himself a mutant, led the X-Men in an ongoing fight to keep the world safe from evil mutants. Professor X used his special computer, Cerebro, to locate a mutant that was more powerful than any he had seen before.

He told the X-Men to board their plane, the Blackbird, and find the mutant in case it was evil and needed to be stopped!

Once they landed, the X-Men left the plane one by one: Cyclops, who shot beams from his eyes, and his brother, Havok, who could shoot them from his body. Marvel Girl could move things with her mind. Iceman was able to turn himself into frozen water. Angel's wings helped him fly. Polaris could move metal like a magnet. And Beast was, well, a beast!

Before the X-Men had even started looking for the mutant, something terrible sneaked up behind them.

"Behind us, Look! It's. . .it's. . ." warned Polaris.

"Quick, everybody scatter! Get moving before we. . ." Havok cried.

Only Cyclops hadn't seen what was creeping up from behind. And before he had a chance to act, the other X-Men were gone, and he had blacked out!

The next thing Cyclops knew, he was back on the Blackbird. His costume was torn and he felt weak. Then he noticed something: his special visor that kept his rays in check was gone. But then he realized something even worse.

"My eyes!" he cried, "They're normal. . .powerless!"

Then he noticed one more thing: the plane was flying on autopilot. Blackbird was heading back to the X-Men's mansion in New York. And Cyclops couldn't stop it!

Professor X was shocked when the plane landed and Cyclops rushed into the mansion.

"Cyclops, what happened? Where are the others?" he asked.

Cyclops told the professor everything he knew. But before Cyclops had finished his story, his eyes started to glow bright red.

"Quickly, Cyclops!" Professor X cried. "Grab some protective glasses! Your optic powers are returning, and they will be stronger than ever!"

The professor had never before seen the X-Men so thoroughly defeated. Other than Cyclops, he was not sure that anyone on the team was even still alive.

They were his students, his friends; they had become like his family.

Professor X knew what he needed to do.

The professor sat at Cerebro and searched the entire globe for mutants. The only way he would be able to save the X-Men would be to gather together a new group of X-Men. They would be the original team's only hope.

In Germany, Professor X saved Kurt Wagner, called Nightcrawler, from an angry mob.

"I can help you find your true potential," Professor X told him.

And in Canada, Professor X made the hero called Wolverine an offer he couldn't refuse.

"I'm giving you a chance to be a free agent," he told Wolverine.

In Ireland, he found Banshee, who had a powerful sonic scream. In Arizona, he convinced the Apache John Proudstar, called Thunderbird, whose strength was unmatched, to join him. In Japan, he called in the mutant Sunfire.

In Africa he recruited Storm, who could control the weather itself, and in Russia, a man called Colossus, who could turn his body into metal.

Once the team was complete, Professor X introduced the new X-Men to Cyclops.

"You have been called here because the X-Men have disappeared," Cyclops told them. "You seven are our only hope. We need to go back to the island of Krakoa, where they vanished. Then we need to find the original X-Men and the mutant that took them!"

Before long the new X-Men were on Krakoa. As they searched the island, they came across an old temple. Could the mutant they were looking for be based there? The new X-Men didn't waste any time finding out!

When they broke down the temple wall, they found part of what they were looking for. The original X-Men were inside, held captive by strange-looking tubes.

Angel said, "The mutant wanted you to come and bring others with you. It feeds on other mutants' energies. It was all a trap! And worst of all, we came to this island *looking* for a mutant . . .

"But the mutant is the island itself!"

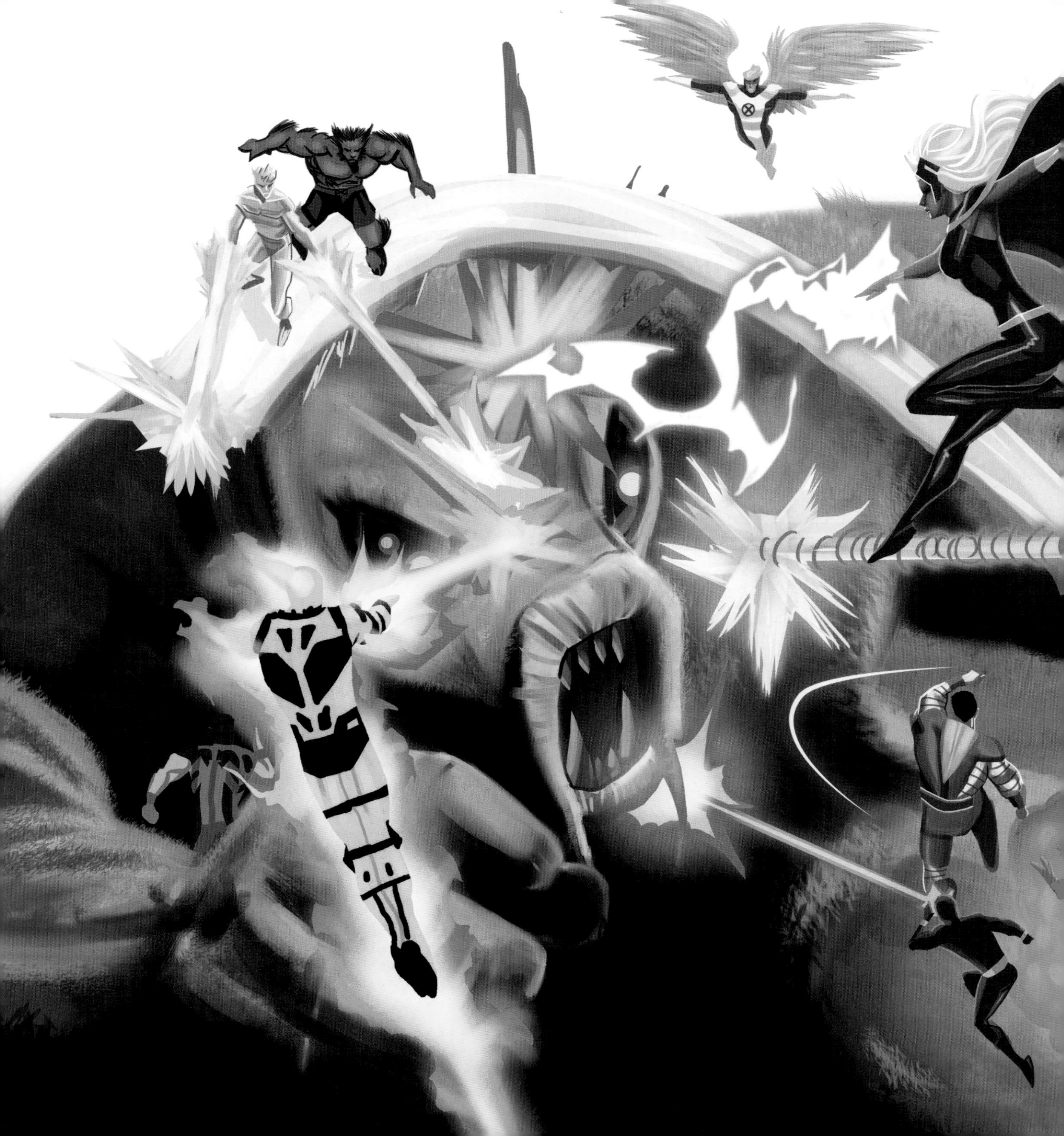

The living island rose up and attacked the X-Men. And in turn, the X-Men, old and new, fought for their lives against their enemy.

Eventually, using their combined powers, they defeated the creature.

Iceman created an ice boat to keep the team afloat, and the sheer force of the X-Men's combined powers sent the island of Krakoa into outer space.

And from that battle a young group of mutant heroes was born—an all-new, all-different team of X-Men!

THE AVENGERS

The Mighty Thor was destined to inherit the throne of Asgard. Thor's brother Loki was very envious, and thought their father, Odin, favored Thor. Loki wanted to stop Thor from becoming king of Asgard and was always thinking of ways to destroy his older brother.

But Thor was smarter than Loki and knew that his younger brother was a troublemaker. Thor asked their father Odin if Loki could be kept prisoner on the Isle of Silence so he wouldn't bother him or attempt to steal the throne.

Loki was very upset. He didn't want to be banished to the Isle of Silence. Since Loki had the power to make people see things that weren't really there and also to send his spirit to places his body could not go, he decided to use both of these powers to attack Thor.

Loki had an idea. He knew that Thor was living on Earth as Dr. Don Blake, and that Earth was filled with heroes. He knew that if he could find one that humans didn't trust — one that was strong enough to defeat his brother — then he could ruin Thor. Loki found Hulk. Hulk could cause lots of damage.

Loki closed his eyes and sent his spirit to Earth to find Hulk, who was walking near some train tracks.

"I will use my powers to make it look like the train is about to crash," Loki said to himself.

Hulk quickly noticed and jumped on the tracks to stop the train from crashing. But because the train wasn't really in danger, the passengers thought Hulk was attacking them.

"Hulk help!" Hulk shouted, but nobody heard. Hulk rushed away from the scene and went to hide.

Just as Loki expected, Dr. Don Blake heard the news of the Hulk's attack and quickly made his transformation into Thor. He had to save people from Hulk. He grabbed his mighty hammer, Mjolnir, and flew off to find Hulk.

What Loki didn't expect was for other heroes to hear the news and leap into action. Billionaire Tony Stark had also learned about Hulk. He quickly put on his Iron Man armor and rushed to the scene.

Dr. Henry Pym and Janet Van Dyne, also known as Ant-Man and Wasp, shrank to their Super-Hero size and also hurried off to save the day. They all met by the train.

"Look at those handprints," the conductor told the team of Super Heroes. "You need to stop him before he hurts more people."

"We can do it," Iron Man assured him.

Loki was watching from above and was very upset. He knew that Hulk couldn't fight four Super Heroes. He just wanted Hulk to fight Thor.

Loki created an image of Hulk that only Thor could see. The mighty Thor cornered who he thought was Hulk and launched his hammer, but the hammer just went through the image. Thor realized that Hulk wasn't really there.

"Loki," Thor said aloud. "You are back to your old tricks."

Thor knew that Hulk wasn't to blame. But instead of telling the others, he went to Asgard to find and fight his brother.

Meanwhile, the Super Heroes were still on the hunt to find Hulk. They had no idea that everything that was happening was Loki's fault and Hulk was innocent.

Then a swarm of ants signaled to Ant-Man that they had found Hulk. The team quickly followed the ants and found him at a nearby circus. Hulk saw the heroes and disguised himself as a circus performer. But the heroes weren't so easily fooled and started to battle Hulk.

Thor raced over the bridge to Asgard as fast as he could. As he entered the Isle of Silence, he knew justice had to be served.

But Loki was expecting his brother. He called upon the Silent Ones who lived belowground to attack Thor.

Thor was able to defeat the Silent Ones and grabbed Loki.

"You won't get away with this, Loki," Thor said as he carried Loki back across the Bifrost bridge and down to Earth, where Loki would face all of the Super Heroes, even Hulk.

When they found the other Super Heroes, Thor cried out, “Don’t hurt Hulk! This is who you should blame. My evil brother Loki. He tricked us into thinking Hulk was the bad guy.”

Loki had one last trick. He used his powers to make it look like there were many of him, and the heroes didn’t know whom to fight. A group of Lokis surrounded Hulk and taunted him. To win the battle, Hulk had to figure out which one was the real Loki.

Hulk found the real Loki. He had to be stopped. He could not rule Asgard. Hulk, along with Iron Man, Thor, Ant-Man, and Wasp, stood up to Loki.

Hulk pushed him to the ground. Loki had no more tricks. They were able to capture this villain.

The heroes had stopped Loki. They couldn't do it alone, but they could do it together as a team. They decided to band together to fight any threat that was too powerful for just one hero. Earth's mightiest heroes assembled. They called themselves the Avengers, and they stood ready to protect the Earth.